Clay tilted hi
Emma. "Wan

She shouldn't say yes, shouldn't encourage this to continue with everything that was still unsaid. And even if everything was out in the open between them, she wasn't sure if her heart was ready. It had been so bruised and battered, she didn't know if it would ever heal.

Yet…she wanted to walk alone with him. Wanted to explore the possibilities and feel *something* again.

"Okay," she said quietly.

Clay stood and offered his hand to her. She took it and he helped her stand, but he didn't let it go as they moved around the fire and toward the lake walk.

Neither spoke for a few moments, though Emma had so many things she wanted to say.

It was Clay who finally broke the silence. "I know we just met, but I really like you, Emma, and I don't think I'm hiding it well. I hope we'll be able to see each other after the wedding."

"I hope we can see each other, too," she said.

But she had a secret that would tear at his heart, just as it had hers…

Gabrielle Meyer lives in central Minnesota on the banks of the Mississippi River with her husband and four young children. As an employee of the Minnesota Historical Society, she fell in love with the rich history of her state and enjoys writing fictional stories inspired by real people and events. Gabrielle can be found at www.gabriellemeyer.com, where she writes about her passion for history, Minnesota and her faith.

Books by Gabrielle Meyer

Love Inspired

Visit the Author Profile page at LoveInspired.com for more titles.

The Baby Secret

Gabrielle Meyer

LOVE INSPIRED

INSPIRATIONAL ROMANCE

LOVE INSPIRED®

INSPIRATIONAL ROMANCE

Recycling programs
for this product may
not exist in your area.

ISBN-13: 978-1-335-58660-5

The Baby Secret

For questions and comments about the quality of this book, please contact us
at CustomerService@Harlequin.com.

Love Inspired
22 Adelaide St. West, 41st Floor
Toronto, Ontario M5H 4E3, Canada
www.LoveInspired.com

Printed in U.S.A.

Thou hast turned for me my mourning into dancing: thou hast put off my sackcloth, and girded me with gladness; To the end that my glory may sing praise to thee, and not be silent. O Lord my God, I will give thanks unto thee for ever.
—*Psalm* 30:11–12

For Elliot Gosiak and Oliver Gosiak,
two sweet boys who mean the world to me.

Chapter One

Sunshine sparkled off the glimmering water of Lake Madeline as Clay Foster stepped out of his SUV to survey Lakepoint Lodge. The sound of children laughing and playing at the beach mingled with the wind as it blew through the tall pine trees surrounding the massive resort.

Taking a deep breath, Clay stood for a moment, allowing the knowledge that he was finally on vacation to sink into his weary mind and heart. It had been a long, devastating year, and he was ready for a little rest and relaxation. If taking a six-month-old baby to a resort was relaxing.

"Welcome to Lakepoint Lodge." An eager teenage boy in khaki shorts and a green polo shirt with a name tag reading Alex approached Clay. "Can I help you with your bags?"

Clay smiled at the bellhop. "You don't know what you're offering. I think I brought half the house with me." He nodded toward the back of his vehicle. "There's a lot."

"That's what I'm here for." Alex grinned and went around to the back of Clay's SUV to lift the hatch. "Is this your first time at Lakepoint Lodge?"

"Yes." Clay closed his door and went to the other side of the SUV to open the back door. Willow had slept all the way up to the resort, which had made for a quiet ride. She was still sleeping, though he didn't expect that to last for long. After he unlatched her car seat, he grabbed the backpack that doubled as the diaper bag and closed the door.

"How long are you staying?" Alex asked.

The boy was trying to make small talk, but Clay was tired. It had been a long week at the clinic where he had recently started his medical practice, and Willow hadn't slept well the night before. However, he was on vacation now and he was sure to get a lot of questions.

Raising a baby as a single father often caused curiosity.

"I'll be here for eight days." Clay took a deep breath, appreciating the fresh air. "My cousin is getting married here a week from today, but

I thought I would come early and take a little vacation before the celebration begins."

"Are you here for the Holt-and-Conner wedding?" Alex asked, his affable personality contagious.

"That's the one."

"You're not the only one who came early." Alex grabbed a couple of suitcases, though there was also a portable high chair, activity station, stroller and pack and play crib that would still need to bc unloaded. "The maid of honor just came in about an hour ago. She'll be here for the whole week, too."

"Oh?" Clay couldn't help glancing around at the dozens of people meandering around the resort, though he didn't know who he was looking for. He'd never met the maid of honor and only knew she was the bride's sister and her name was Emma. The engagement had been so quick, Clay hadn't had time to meet many of the bride's friends or family. "I'll have to find her and introduce myself."

"I'll come back for the other stuff later," Alex said as he closed the back hatch and led the way to the lodge.

They entered the main doors, and Clay felt transported back in time. The lodge had a placard that said it had been built in 1947, with a historic photo of the resort near the front doors. The lobby had high ceilings with thick beams, a massive rock fireplace, pine-plank floors and board-and-batten walls made of pine and darkened over time. Oversize furniture flanked the fireplace, and a registration desk stretched across the back of the room. A few people were sitting in the lobby, playing games, reading or just visiting.

"Here she is," Alex said to Clay.

"Who?" Clay asked, turning his attention away from the architecture of the building.

"The maid of honor."

Clay looked around the room and finally saw an attractive woman walking down the wide staircase. At first, he thought it was the bride, Carrie—but as she drew closer, the differences between the sisters grew more obvious. Emma was small and cute, with large brown eyes, a round face and a dimple in her chin. Her dark brown hair was long and thick, and she wore it up in a high ponytail.

She was beautiful, a fact that didn't fail to register in Clay's trampled heart. It had been almost five months since his ex-wife, Sadie, had left him, and in all that time, Clay hadn't let himself notice whether or not another woman was attractive. Until now.

His life was too complicated to even think about romance.

Emma looked like she was on her way to the beach. She was wearing a long sundress over a swimsuit and carried a beach bag on her shoulder. When she glanced at Clay, she offered him a smile but didn't appear to know who he was. It didn't surprise him, since he wouldn't have known her, either, if the bellhop hadn't pointed her out.

Should he introduce himself? Or let her go and make introductions later?

"Miss Holt," Alex called out to her with a big grin. "This man is here for the wedding, too."

Emma stopped and looked at Clay a bit closer, a curious smile on her face.

They were going to be introduced after all.

"Hi," Clay said, extending his right hand to shake hers. "I'm Clay Foster, Jack's cousin and best man."

Emma's curious smile turned into a beautiful grin. If he'd thought she was attractive before, seeing her smile made her even more so. "It's nice to finally meet you. I'm Emma Holt, Carrie's sister and the maid of honor. Or matron of honor—I'm not sure how that works."

Matron of honor? That probably meant she

was married. For some reason, the thought disappointed Clay.

Willow began to fuss, and Clay glanced down, remembering to introduce her. "This is my daughter, Willow."

Emma smiled at the baby. "Hello, Willow." She looked up at Clay. "She's beautiful."

"Thank you." He couldn't take credit for Willow's beauty—but it seemed the appropriate thing to say. "I didn't know you'd be here early."

"It was a last-minute decision." Emma glanced at the baby again, frowning just slightly, as if something puzzled her, though she seemed to put the thought aside quickly and met Clay's gaze again. "I thought it was time I took a little vacation. And I promised Carrie I'd get a few things done for the wedding while I'm here. I'm going to meet with the wedding planner, and I have a whole bag full of wedding programs that need to be folded and place cards that need to be filled out."

Clay glanced at Emma's bags and then out the windows toward the sparkling lake. "Are you headed to the beach?"

"I am. You're more than welcome to join me, if you'd like. I'll be there for a while."

Clay's pulse beat a little harder than normal at Emma's invitation—a strange sensation he hadn't been expecting. For five months, he'd been mourning the loss of his wife and caring for their daughter single-handedly. He hadn't thought about dating or relationships, and though Emma's invitation wasn't romantic in nature, was it wise to spend time with the first woman who made his pulse skitter? Especially when she might be married?

"Thanks for the invitation," Clay said as he looked toward the registration counter, where he needed to check in. "I'll see how long it takes us to get settled. I'm sure we'll be bumping into each other a lot this week."

"I hope so." Emma smiled again and then left the lodge.

Clay forced himself to walk toward the counter, where he was greeted by an older woman with a name tag that said Marilyn Butler.

"Welcome to Lakepoint Lodge," Marilyn said.

"This gentleman is here for the wedding." Alex set Clay's bags down by the counter.

"Oh." Marilyn smiled. "Dr. Clay Foster? I have you checking in for eight nights?"

"Yes." Clay returned her smile. "That's correct."

"Both you and Miss Holt are here for the wedding—the woman you were just speaking to." Marilyn started typing something into the computer. "Since you're both here for the wedding, I've put you in neighboring suites on the second floor with a beautiful view of the lake. I'm sure the two of you have some things to get ready for the wedding. My daughter, Liv, is the wedding planner, and she said she'll be meeting with Emma on Monday morning."

Clay's curiosity about Emma was piqued. Marilyn and Alex had called Emma *Miss* Holt. Did that mean she was single after all? Then why the comment about being a matron of honor?

"Will your wife be joining you, Dr. Foster?"

"No." Clay shook his head, not interested in sharing more information than necessary, though he had come to expect questions. "My ex-wife and I are divorced. It will just be Willow and me here this week."

"Are you raising that baby girl all on your own?" Marilyn's eyes grew round. "You poor man."

Clay hated pity even more than he disliked people prying into his personal affairs.

If Marilyn knew the truth, she'd give him more than pity. She'd be appalled on his behalf.

Clay had learned about Sadie's infidelity a year ago. They had worked through the affair and she had promised it was over, but then he'd learned she was pregnant.

With the other man's child.

It had taken everything in Clay to stay and fight for his marriage. He couldn't give up on them, and he couldn't blame the baby. But a month after Willow had been born, and Clay had been coming to terms with raising another man's child, he had arrived home from work to find that Sadie had moved out. A babysitter had been with Willow and a handwritten note had been on their bed. Sadie was leaving him and the baby. She had fallen in love with someone else and the new boyfriend hadn't wanted the child, so she had chosen to abandon them.

To this day, Clay didn't know the identity of Willow's biological father and he didn't want to know. It was easier to raise her as his own that way. On the day Sadie had left, he'd decided that he and Willow would write their own story. They'd both been abandoned and deceived by Sadie, but it didn't have to define their lives.

"Do you have a nanny or some other childcare provider with you?" Marilyn asked.

"No."

"We have a childcare program here. You're welcome to use it both day and night, whenever you'd like—just let me know. You deserve some relaxation, too."

"I'm sure I'll take you up on the offer."

"I hope you do." Marilyn completed the registration process and then said, "Alex will take your bags up to your room." She motioned for the bellhop to grab Clay's bags. "There's a dance in the ballroom downstairs tonight, so get rested up this afternoon."

A dance? Clay had no desire to go to a dance with a bunch of strangers. Attending the wedding next week was going to be hard enough with all his family and friends there. He hadn't felt much like dancing or celebrating in the past year, but he would for Jack and Carrie.

"Thank you," Clay said as he took his key. It was connected to a key chain shaped like a pine tree with the room number 202. He couldn't remember the last time he'd stayed at a hotel or lodge with a real key.

Clay followed Alex up the set of stairs and across a long hallway. They stopped at his room and he opened the door. After Alex deposited his bags, he told Clay that he'd be back with the rest of Willow's stuff and then left the room.

The suite had a small kitchenette and a living room with a gas fireplace. A door led into the bedroom, but it was the large window and sliding glass door in the living room, looking out at the lake, that drew his attention. A little balcony beckoned him. He unlocked the door and slid it open and then stepped out onto the balcony, still carrying Willow in her car seat.

Lake Madeline spread out before him in all its glory. It was one of the largest and prettiest lakes in Minnesota and a perfect location for Carrie and Jack's outdoor wedding.

The main lodge dominated the property, sitting on a point on Lake Madeline. There were dozens of smaller log cabins along the shoreline and other buildings dotting his view. One looked like a boathouse, another had a sign that said Bait Shop and another that said Candy Shop.

The beach was close enough that Clay could make out at least twenty people in the water and on the sand. One person, in particular, drew his attention.

Emma was sitting on a large beach towel and wearing a floppy hat.

Maybe it wouldn't be a bad idea to join her for a little bit and get to know the maid of honor. After all, they were going to be seeing a lot of each other, and what was the harm in making a new friend?

And finding out if she was married?

After he fed and changed Willow, they'd head to the beach.

* * *

Emma closed her eyes and allowed the sound of the water lapping against the shore to ease her mind. It was so peaceful here at the resort. She couldn't believe she hadn't thought about getting away before now. The past twelve months had been the hardest of her life, and she was ready for a vacation.

It had begun a year ago when Tyler had revealed his affair to her. A month later, while they'd been separated, he had been diagnosed with pancreatic cancer. He'd only lived for three more months, making her a widow eight months ago. It had happened so quickly, she was just now coming to terms with it all.

"Hey," said a male voice. "Mind if I join you?"

Emma glanced up and saw Clay Foster standing on the edge of the beach in a pair of swimming shorts and flip-flops. He held his daughter on one hip and had a bag slung over his shoulder.

Her pulse ticked up a notch at seeing him again, but she managed to smile.

"Sure." She sat up and motioned to the empty spot next to her. "Pull up a beach towel and have a seat."

Emma watched as he wrestled a towel out of his bag and laid it down with one hand.

"Here," she said as she helped him settle it on the sand.

"Thanks. It's amazing what you can—and can't—do with a baby in your arms." He set the baby on the towel and then took a seat next to her, pulling toys out of the bag to place near Willow.

Clay was tall, with broad shoulders and a trim waist. His dark brown hair and eyes were attractive, but it was his smile, and the dimple in his right cheek, that instantly made Emma like him. That and the way he cared for his baby.

She glanced around, looking for his wife, but saw no one in tow.

He must have seen her curious gaze because he said, "I'm here alone."

Warmth filled her cheeks. "Sorry—do you get that question a lot?"

"More than you can imagine."

"So, it's just you and the baby, then?"

He nodded. "I'm a single dad—not something I ever thought I'd say."

The little one grabbed a toy and instantly brought it to her mouth.

"She's adorable."

"Thanks." He grinned. "Though I don't know why I keep taking credit for her adorableness." He pulled out sunscreen and began to lather it on his daughter as he glanced at Emma. "I'm surprised we haven't met yet."

"It's probably because everything happened so fast for Carrie and Jack. How long have they been dating? Like six months? My life has been kind of chaotic, and I haven't had a chance to spend much time with them."

That would also explain why she hadn't known that the best man was an attractive single dad. Emma would have to ask Carrie why she hadn't mentioned it.

Clay nodded, a little pensive. "Jack and Carrie met around the same time Willow was born, so I was a little preoccupied, too."

"If I remember correctly from Carrie, you're a doctor?" Emma asked.

"I am." He nodded. "Just recently started my family practice in St. Cloud. What about you?"

"I'm a nurse practitioner in Timber Falls. I moved there two years ago from St. Cloud to join their medical team."

"Really?" He frowned. "Strange how we've never crossed paths. I suppose you left before I got to St. Cloud."

The two towns were only thirty miles apart, but there were tons of medical professionals in both, so it probably wasn't that strange that they hadn't met.

"I guess our paths crossed when they were meant to." Emma smiled, but for some reason, voicing that statement made her pulse pick up speed again.

"Will your husband join you this week?" he asked, peeking at her left hand, no doubt looking for a ring.

Emma glanced out at the lake and shook her head. She hoped her sunglasses hid the expression in her eyes, though she couldn't help when the edges of her mouth turned down. "My husband passed away eight months ago."

"I'm sorry."

She nodded. "It was a really tough year for a lot of reasons. I kind of feel like I'm just coming out of a fog." Which was an understatement. Tyler's infidelity had come on the heels of her second miscarriage, and she'd hardly had time to grieve the loss when she'd learned about his affair. She had decided to take back her maiden name, Holt, and start over as best she could.

"We've had a pretty tough year, too," Clay said. "My wife left me for another man soon after Willow was born, and I've been adjusting to being a single dad."

"Now *I'm* sorry." She looked at him. "I can't imagine what you've been through."

She felt a bond with Clay, if only because of their shared sorrow. She hated to think of anyone suffering the way he had, but she took comfort in knowing she wasn't alone.

"It was supposed to be a happy time for us," he continued. "We had just purchased a big Victorian fixer-upper. Sadie had been living in it for several months as I completed residency in Minneapolis. She was working as the general manager of a hotel in St. Cloud, but when I finally moved in, I realized she had been having an affair."

Emma's breath stilled, and she slowly lowered her sunglasses. "What did you say was her name?"

"Sadie."

For a moment, Emma was afraid her heart would stop beating. His ex-wife's name was Sadie—and she was the general manager of a hotel in St. Cloud? Was it possible that Clay's ex-wife was the same Sadie Tyler had been seeing?

It couldn't be possible. What were the odds?

When Emma had finally learned the truth from Tyler, he had admitted he'd met the woman at a hotel in St. Cloud while he'd been there for a pharmaceutical conference. She was the general manager. The affair had lasted for several months before Emma had caught on. But when she had, it had been the most devastating time in her life. She had left Tyler and moved in with her sister, Carrie, but Tyler had come begging for her to forgive him.

Emma had been ready to call it quits, but then Tyler had been diagnosed with cancer and she couldn't leave his side. She had stayed with him through his treatment and been there at the end. He had asked her to forgive him, and she had, though the pain of his betrayal still lingered.

"Her name is Sadie Foster," Clay repeated. "At least, it was. I think she took her maiden name back." He frowned. "Did you know her?"

Sadie Foster. Emma's stomach turned, and she was afraid she'd be sick. She would never forget that name for as long as she lived. But did Clay know that Tyler was the man Sadie had been seeing?

Emma had to control her features so they wouldn't betray her. If he didn't know, Emma had no wish to tell him. What was the point? It would only cause more pain.

"I didn't know her," Emma said, shaking her head and looking down at the baby, who was playing with a toy and blowing raspberry bubbles from her mouth. "I recognize the name, though." She couldn't lie to him. No doubt he was just as sick of the lies as she was.

Clay also looked at his daughter. "I don't know if I'll ever recover from what happened to us—but I'm trying to make a fresh start with Willow."

It was as if he could read her mind. "Same here." She was quiet for a second and then said, "Do you think it'll ever get any easier?"

With a heavy sigh, Clay nodded. "I hope and pray it does."

Emma couldn't believe that their pasts were so intricately entwined, even though they'd never met. Their spouses had betrayed both of them—together—and left Clay and Emma to pick up the pieces.

She felt drawn to Clay because of it, even if he didn't know the extent of the situation. He didn't know that her husband had cheated on her—only that he had died eight months ago. She didn't want to burden him with the rest of her sad story.

And she didn't want the truth to hinder their week. If anything, she longed to help Clay enjoy his time at the resort. Give him something to smile about again. And maybe, if she could get him to smile, she might have a reason to smile, too.

"I have an idea," Emma said, forcing her voice to sound lighter than she felt. "If you're like me, you probably came here to get away from the past for a while."

He glanced up at her, his features softening. "That's exactly what I had hoped."

"Then let's have a great week and try to forget about all of it. I heard there's a dance tonight. I wasn't going to go because I didn't know anyone, but now I do." She smiled at him. "Do you like to dance?"

Clay chuckled and shook his head. "Not when I don't have to."

"Really?" She tried not to sound disappointed. She hadn't even wanted to go before, but now she couldn't think of a better way to keep her mind off their troubles. "I love to dance—with the right people. We need to warm up for the wedding dance next weekend, don't we? What do you say?"

His brown eyes sparkled as he shook his head, but Emma could see he was getting ready to concede. "I don't have any fancy moves."

She laughed. "Neither do I. But that's the fun of dancing. Anyone can do it, and you don't have to be fancy."

He gave her a look that said otherwise. "I can't be held responsible if you feel embarrassed dancing with me once you see how bad I am."

"I don't know anyone here, so I won't be embarrassed."

"Don't say I didn't warn you."

Emma smiled. "I won't—I promise."

A companionable silence slipped between them, broken by Willow, who started to scoot off the towel, heading for the sand.

"Would you like to join us in the water?" Clay asked as he scooped her up. "Willow has never been swimming in a lake before."

"I would love to." Emma tried to smile again, but it fell flat as she watched Clay holding his daughter.

Her heart constricted with unexpected grief, and she wondered how different her life would be right now if she and Tyler had been able to have a baby. They'd tried for years, and each miscarriage had left a gaping hole in her heart.

She forced the thoughts away, choosing instead to be happy in this moment, experiencing a first with Willow.

Clay walked to the edge of the lake and stepped into the water until it went up to his ankles. Emma took off her sundress and followed, feeling the cool water on her toes.

Willow squealed with delight as Clay set her

toes into the water. At first, she raised both her feet and then slowly lowered them back down. Soon she was splashing the water, giggling and gurgling with approval.

"Let's go out a little farther," Clay said as he moved into the water. When he was about waist-deep, he lowered Willow in slowly, to let her adjust.

"I think she likes it," Emma said with a smile.

Willow splashed the water with her chubby little hands, getting both Emma's and Clay's faces wet in the process. They both laughed.

The difference between Clay's dark brown eyes and Willow's blue ones was startling in the sunshine, and Emma couldn't help but ask, "Does her mother have those brilliant blue eyes, too?"

Clay didn't answer for a couple seconds as he moved Willow in the water. Finally, he shook his head. "No. Sadie's eyes are as brown as mine."

Emma frowned. What were the odds that a baby would have bright blue eyes when her parents both had brown? She remembered something about recessive genes that caused blue eyes from her high school biology, but it was vague.

"They're such a pretty shade of blue," Emma said, trying to cover the awkwardness of the moment. "My husband—"

She paused, realizing what she was about to say.

Tyler's eyes had been that exact same shade of blue. She'd noticed it when she'd seen the baby for the first time inside, and it had made her pause. Tyler's blue eyes had been one of the things that had initially attracted her to him. She could remember, in vivid detail, the moment he'd looked at her for the first time across the commons in their dormitory at college. She had never seen eyes so bright or brilliant.

Until now.

A sick feeling started in the pit of Emma's stomach and it soon turned to a cold sweat as she started to put all the pieces together.

Tyler had begun his affair with Sadie Foster last February—sixteen months ago. Emma had learned about it in June—twelve months ago. And Willow was six months old.

Was Willow Tyler's baby? It was completely possible.

Emma was afraid she was going to lose her lunch right there at the beach, in front of Clay and everyone else. Dread and devastation filled her with panic. She had to get away from there. Had to sort out her feelings and try to make sense of it all.

Willow couldn't be Tyler's baby—she just couldn't.

Clay glanced at Emma and frowned. "Are you okay? You look a little pale."

The cold sweat had turned to a burning sensation racing through her body. "I don't feel well," she said as she put her hands to her cheeks. They were on fire. "I think I should head into the lodge and lie down."

Clay lifted Willow out of the water, concern tightening his features. "Do you need me to get you anything?"

"No." She shook her head and started to move out of the lake. Her feet felt like they were tied to gigantic anchors, and each step she took was torture. She just needed to get away.

"I can help," Clay said as he followed her out of the water. "Are you diabetic? Hypoglycemic?"

"I'm fine," Emma said, reaching for her towel and sundress. "I just need to lie down. It was nice to meet you."

"Can I check on you a little later?"

"That won't be necessary." She couldn't look at him—couldn't look at the baby. If she did, she was afraid she'd see some of Tyler's other features.

"Let me know if you need anything," he said as she walked away. "I'm in room 202."

Emma lifted a hand in acknowledgment but kept walking toward the lodge, her heart beating so fast she thought she might have a heart attack right there on the lawn.

Tears stung her eyes, even as she tried to talk sense to herself. Maybe the baby wasn't Tyler's—maybe it was a coincidence that she had the same color eyes.

But even as she thought it, she knew it was all adding up to be true, and her empty arms stung with awareness. She hadn't been able to have a baby—Tyler's baby—but he had given one to Sadie Foster. And then Sadie had abandoned that baby, and Clay was now raising her as his own.

Did he know the truth? Would he be more devastated than she was to learn that his daughter wasn't his biological child?

Suddenly, it was all too much, and Emma raced for her room.

Chapter Two

Clay stood on the beach staring after Emma, concerned and curious about her behavior. She didn't strike him as a dramatic kind of person, and she really had looked sick before she'd left his side. His medical training went into overdrive as he thought about the visual symptoms he had observed. Sallow skin and a cold sweat, followed by bright red cheeks and watery eyes. She'd looked like she'd been about to vomit—and maybe that was why she had started to run to the lodge.

He wanted to be available for her, if she needed him. But first, he had to put Willow down for her nap.

Clay didn't waste any time wiping Willow off with the beach towel and packing up their things. Willow fussed as he put her into a dry diaper and clothes. She tried to wiggle away as she reached for the lake.

"We'll come back again," he promised his daughter. "But right now you need a nap and we need to see if our new friend needs help."

As he walked back to the lodge, Willow's head started to bob on his shoulder, and he knew she'd be ready for a bottle and bed soon. Thankfully, she was like clockwork and maintained a pretty regular schedule. It helped that she had a full-time nanny who ensured that the schedule was followed when Clay was at work.

"Is Miss Holt going to be okay?" Marilyn asked from behind the registration counter when Clay entered the lodge. "She looked practically green as she ran through here."

"I'm not sure," Clay said, stopping to talk to the owner of the lodge. "Did she go upstairs?"

"Yes—she's in room 204, right next to yours."

Clay smiled, thankful for the information, though he was certain it violated some sort of privacy policy. Marilyn Butler didn't seem to be the kind of person to pay attention to such details.

"I'll check on her in a little while," Clay said. "Hopefully it's a passing ailment."

"You do that, Dr. Foster. And if anyone else

has any complaints, I'll send them your way, too."

He tried not to show his dismay at her comment—after all, he wasn't supposed to be on duty and the last thing he needed on vacation was more work. But he was a family doctor first and foremost, and if anyone was in need, he would never turn them away. Instead of responding with a comment, he simply smiled and went upstairs.

The hallway was dark except for the dim light of the wall sconces. Clay walked to 204 and listened for a moment, trying to hear if Emma was in distress.

He couldn't hear anything, and Willow was starting to fuss, so he went into his room and set her in the activity center he had brought from home.

She started to cry so loud, Clay was afraid she would bother Emma next door, so he worked quickly in the kitchenette to make her bottle.

"Shh," Clay said to his daughter. "Just a minute, sweetie."

When he was done, he took her into the bedroom and sat on the rocking chair in the corner to feed her.

She immediately quieted and took the bottle as she looked up at him.

Her blue eyes were so beautiful and innocent. Emma's question about her eyes had troubled him because he'd always suspected that
Willow's eye color was from her biological
father, and Clay wasn't about to tell her the
truth about that part of his story. Only a couple people knew that Willow wasn't his flesh
and blood, and he wanted to keep it that way.
One day, he would tell Willow, but he'd leave
it up to her whether or not she wanted to look
for her birth father.

Slowly, Willow's eyes began to close, but she
continued to drink her bottle. Clay had to stop
her midway to burp her and she cried again,
but afterward she kept on eating and was soon
fast asleep.

He pulled away the empty bottle, and her
little lips kept sucking a few more times before she was still. Clay stood and set her in the
pack and play in his room, turned on the video
monitor that was connected to his phone and
went into the living room, closing the door behind him.

It was good to have a bit of time to himself. He had planned to read some books this
week—but it was difficult to concentrate when
he was worried about Emma.

Clay's phone began to ring, so he walked out

to the balcony and saw that it was his cousin. "Hello, Jack."

"Hey, buddy!" Jack said a second later. "Did you remember to call the tuxedo place and give them your final measurements?"

"I did one better. I already picked up my tuxedo. I have it with me at Lakepoint."

"That's right. I forgot you were heading up there early."

"Is he already at the lodge?" Carrie asked in the background.

"Yeah," Jack responded. "I forgot to mention that to you."

"My sister is there, too," Carrie said. "Turn on the speakerphone."

A couple of seconds later, Carrie said, "Hey, Clay! My sister was heading to Lakepoint Lodge today, too. You'll have to look her up."

Clay leaned on the railing as he surveyed the lake. "I already met her. We ran into each other right when I got here."

"Oh, that's cool. I had no idea you were going to be there, too. I think you guys will hit it off. She's had a pretty rough year, but she seems to be turning a corner. Her husband passed away—"

"She mentioned it to me." He stood straight again and glanced at the neighboring balcony, realizing that Emma might be able to hear his conversation. Going back inside, he spoke in a softer voice. "We were in the lake with Willow, and Emma suddenly looked sick. She excused herself and ran back to the lodge. I'm concerned about her, but she wouldn't let me help."

"Maybe I should call her and see if she needs anything." Carrie's voice held concern.

Clay felt relief as he nodded. "That would be great. She might respond to you better than me. I just wanted to make sure she was okay."

"That's nice of you," Carrie said. "I was looking forward to the two of you meeting. I think you'll have a lot in common."

He could hear a matchmaker tone to her voice, and he didn't like it. Family members, friends and coworkers had started to hint that he should get back out there and date again, but he'd turned each of them away. He and Sadie had been together for almost twelve years—besides, he wasn't interested in letting someone pulverize his heart again. Marriage, dating and romance were behind him, and he was planning to focus on raising his daughter.

"Let me know if I can help Emma," he said. "Or if you two need anything else for the wedding. I'm here and can run errands if need be."

"Thanks," Carrie said. "I'll let you know, and if not, we'll talk to you on Thursday, when we get to the lodge."

"Okay. See you guys later."

"Bye," Jack and Carrie said at the same time.

Clay hung up the phone, but he still felt unsettled. Something was wrong with Emma, and he wouldn't rest easy until he knew she was okay.

It had been several hours since Emma had been at the beach with Clay and Willow. Her sister had tried calling her a few times, but Emma had texted back and said she couldn't talk. When Carrie responded and asked if she was feeling okay, Emma guessed that Clay had talked to her. She wasn't ready to tell her sister what she suspected, so she had simply told Carrie that she was fine and not to worry about her.

But Emma wasn't fine. She had been sitting in the living room of her suite, staring out at the lake. Though the past year had been devastating, she had been meeting with her pastor on a regular basis to talk through her pain, and she felt like she had been making good progress—until now.

What would it mean if Tyler had had a child? Emma couldn't even wrap her mind around something that life shaking. But maybe Willow wasn't Tyler's baby. That was definitely a possibility. After all, Sadie and Clay had been married at the time.

A spark of hope filled her chest as she latched on to that prospect. Maybe her worrying was for nothing. If she could somehow ask Clay—or get him talking—perhaps she could find the truth.

But that led her back to her previous concerns. What if Willow *was* Tyler's baby and Clay didn't even know?

There was only one way to find out, and that was to talk to Clay.

Her stomach had settled as she'd come to terms with the possibilities—and now she was hungry. She had missed lunch and supper, and the dance would be starting soon. Maybe Clay would still be willing to go, if she hadn't scared him off completely.

Emma grabbed a granola bar from her bag and ate it as she went into the bedroom and pulled her suitcase onto the bed. She had brought several semiformal outfits for the wedding events, so it wasn't hard to find something appropriate for a dance.

She opted for a simple black A-line dress. It was sleeveless and had an Audrey Hepburn–

vintage feel. The skirt was free-flowing and would be good for dancing, though she still didn't feel much like kicking up her heels tonight. All she could think about was Willow.

The phone on the nightstand began to ring, surprising Emma. She hadn't had a landline since she was a kid and only used her cell phone. To hear the ring of a real rotary phone made her smile.

"Hello?" she said as she picked it up.

"Hey—is this Emma?" a male voice asked on the other end.

"Yes."

"It's Clay—I hope you don't mind that I called. Marilyn patched me through to your room."

Emma sat on the bed, her knees a little weak at hearing his voice again. "It's okay." She licked her lips, which were suddenly dry. "I'm sorry I dashed out on you earlier today."

"That's partly why I'm calling. I hope you're feeling better. I've been worried about you all afternoon."

She smiled. "I appreciate that. I am feeling better. Thanks."

He paused for a second. "I was also wondering if you were still up to going to the dance. It's been a pretty uneventful afternoon over here.

I thought I needed a little peace and quiet—but I'm realizing that I also need to have some fun. I signed Willow up for childcare tonight and thought I'd check out the dance. Want to come?"

Her chest filled with warmth at the knowledge that he wanted to spend more time with her.

"I would like that. I still need to get ready—but I can meet you downstairs in about twenty minutes."

"That's perfect. I'll head down and get Willow situated in childcare and then wait for you in the lobby."

"See you then." She hung up the phone and took a deep breath. Nerves fluttered in her stomach—not only because she needed to talk to Clay about Willow but because this was as close to a date as she had been on in ten years. It wasn't a date—not really—but she was getting dressed up and meeting a handsome man to go to a dance. For all intents and purposes, it felt like a date.

She quickly went into the bathroom, washed her face, put on some makeup and styled her hair into an updo with tendrils curling around her face.

Before leaving her room, she pulled her strappy silver heels out of her suitcase and slipped them on. One quick look in the full-length mirror on the back of the door told her she was ready. Her cheeks were pink and her eyes were alight with expectation, though she wasn't sure what she was expecting. She was hopeful Clay could put her fears to rest, even if she wasn't sure how she was going to get him to talk about such a delicate subject. But there had to be a way—and she had to figure it out.

Emma left her room and walked down the darkened hallway to the staircase that led to the lobby.

She hadn't been this nervous in years.

Slowly, she descended the stairs and made her way to the lower level.

As soon as she turned the landing, she saw Clay waiting for her.

And her breath stilled.

He was wearing a dark blue blazer with a white shirt underneath and a pair of blue jeans. His brown hair was combed up and off to one side, and his eyes—oh, his eyes. They were so brown, she could easily get lost in the depths of them, especially when he was looking at her the way he was right now.

A slow smile lifted his lips as he took in her appearance, and Emma felt a charge of electricity run through her. She had never been so aware of someone else before, and she wasn't sure if it was because she was attracted to him or because they shared such raw and intimate heartbreaks. Either way, this feeling she had was one she wanted to cling to because it awakened in her a sense of wholeness or, at the very least, the promise of being whole. She was *feeling* again. Feeling something other than pain.

For a moment, she forgot about Willow and the difficult talk they would need to have. And she just admired Clay.

"You look amazing, Emma," he said as she stopped at the foot of the stairs. "I'm happy to see you have your color back."

"You look good, too." Her cheeks warmed at the praise. She had only just met this man, yet she felt like they'd known each other for years.

"Are you sure you're feeling up to a dance?" he asked.

"I think so."

He motioned to the stairs that led down to the lower level of the lodge. Soft music was drifting up.

"Shall we?" he asked.

Together, they walked down the stairs and entered the ballroom. Large windows faced the lake, with doors between them. It appeared that the space doubled as the dining room, with dozens of tables spread out. On one end, a dance floor was filled with guests as a band played "The Way You Look Tonight."

Beyond the windows, the sun was setting on Lake Madeline, and the sky was filled with vibrant red, pink, orange and deep purple. White tablecloths covered the tables, and soft light glistened from small votive candles. The delicate tinkling of laughter filled the room and intermingled with the gentle cadence of the song.

"The wedding reception will be held in here?" Clay asked Emma.

"Yes—but I think the dance will be out on the patio if the weather is nice. I'm meeting with the wedding planner this week to go over last-minute details for Carrie. The wedding planner is a friend from church, and also the daughter of the owners here at Lakepoint Lodge. She's the one who told me about this place, and I suggested it to Carrie and Jack."

"I was wondering why they had chosen this resort. I think it'll make a great place for their wedding." He smiled and indicated the refreshment table. "Hungry?"

"I'm starving." Emma would need some fortification for the talk she intended to have with Clay.

They walked over to the table where a charcuterie board was laid out with cheeses, olives, grapes, crackers and nuts. After they both filled their plates, they walked to a small table in the corner of the room where it wasn't quite so loud.

Emma took a seat across from Clay at the two-person table. The candlelight flickered in his dark brown eyes as he smiled at her. He carried himself with confidence, yet there was something very humble about him as well. She worked with a lot of medical professionals, and it didn't take her long to weed out the arrogant ones from those who were truly servants of the people. Clay appeared to be the latter, and she suspected he was a good doctor.

But there was a reason she had come to this dance—and it wasn't to admire Dr. Clay Foster. She needed to know if her late husband was Willow's father. And the only way she was going to find out was if she asked Clay. She couldn't come right out and say what was on her mind, especially if he wasn't aware that Willow might not be his—but she also couldn't sit back and wonder for the rest of her life, either.

She'd have to get up the courage to ask him—and the sooner the better.

Chapter Three

Clay smiled at Emma, feeling as awkward as he had on his first date in high school. He looked down at his plate and shook his head. "Sorry—it's been a while since I've sat across the table from a beautiful woman with candlelight between us and music playing in the background. Not that this is a date," he added quickly. "Just not part of my normal routine anymore."

Her cheeks filled with color as she looked down at her plate. "It's been a while for me, too."

"Having a baby has changed almost every aspect of my life."

She moved some of her food around her plate as she said, "I imagine it's been difficult to take care of a baby all by yourself."

"I can't pretend I'm doing it alone," he admitted. "I have a full-time nanny, and my parents come to St. Cloud as often as they can to help. Sadie's parents have been great, too, although it's tough for them, given the situation. Sadie is from St. Cloud, which is why we moved there, and her parents aren't too far away."

"I'm happy you have help." Emma toyed with one of her olives and seemed to be weighing her words carefully. "Was Willow a surprise pregnancy?"

Had Willow been a surprise? Next to Sadie's infidelity, she'd been the biggest surprise of his life. But how much did he risk telling Emma? She was a stranger—kind of—but she also seemed to be genuinely curious and had a kind nature about her. He couldn't imagine she would use the information to hurt him or his daughter. Still, he couldn't be too careful, for Willow's sake.

Leaning back in his chair, he said, "Willow was not a planned pregnancy, if that's what you mean."

"I just wondered—since your wife left so soon after she was born. I was curious—"

"It's okay." He stopped her. "I know my life isn't normal, and I suppose Willow and I will get a lot of questions as she grows up. For the past five months, we've kept to ourselves a lot.

Some of my colleagues and close friends and family know about our situation, but that's about all. It's only natural that you would wonder."

"I don't want to make you uncomfortable."

"You're not." For reasons he couldn't explain, he wanted to tell Emma more about himself and Willow. It felt good to meet someone who didn't know his past and who was making fresh observations about his life now. Granted, it wasn't what he had planned—but it was his new normal and he was ready to embrace it. "Feel free to ask me anything you'd like."

She looked up at him, studying him with her wide brown eyes. She really was beautiful, especially tonight, with her hair done up and wearing a dress that complemented her attractiveness.

"I'm just curious about Willow," she said. "You mentioned your wife left you for another man. I just wondered—I mean—" She paused, clearly at a loss for words. "Her blue eyes—they're so unlike yours—and…" Again, she paused.

What was she trying to ask him? And why did she want to know? Had she caught on to the fact that Willow wasn't his biological daughter? Was it that obvious? He didn't think so. Yet if she had caught on and was curious, was there harm in telling her the truth?

"Are you wondering if Willow is mine?"

She stopped sputtering her question, and the look in her expressive eyes told him that was *exactly* what she was wondering.

On the day Willow had been born, Clay had decided that no matter what, Willow was going to be his daughter. He was listed on the birth certificate as her father, and she would carry his last name. It didn't matter to him that she had a different biological father. Willow Lillian Foster was his daughter for life. So, as he looked at Emma, he had no qualms saying "Yes, Willow is my daughter."

Something like relief passed over her face, and she lifted her chin a fraction, a smile tilting up her lips. "I'm sorry if I was being presumptuous."

"It's okay. Like I said, our situation is unique, so I'm sure people wonder."

They ate their food as they chatted about their work, and Clay soon realized that he and Emma did have a lot in common. They had read several of the same books, they both enjoyed hiking and playing golf, and they even shared an interest in many of the same bands. Soon they were laughing as Clay told her a story about a hiking trip he'd taken and how he'd come across a skunk that had left an indelible mark.

When the food was gone, he finally got up the nerve to ask her to dance.

"I'd love to," she said as she rose from the table.

It was another slow song, and he felt a bit more confident dancing to something that didn't require fancy footwork or talent.

The band played "Someone to Watch Over Me" as they stepped onto the dance floor. Emma had a delicate stature, but her heels made her taller as they faced each other. He reached for her, putting one hand around the small of her back.

The moment he touched her, he was very aware of everything about her. Her subtle perfume, her slender waist, the way her lips turned up in a gentle smile as she listened to him speak. It felt good to hold someone again—but more than that, it felt good to connect with someone he found interesting and enjoyable. It was easy to be with Emma.

She looked up at him as their hands touched. The music was so soothing and rhythmic, it was easy to get lost in the sound.

They started to dance, and Clay quickly realized how much he liked it.

"See," she teased, "this isn't so bad."

"You make it easy, Emma."

She smiled at him, looking relaxed and happy.

It felt natural to draw Emma closer as they moved around the dance floor. He led and she followed with such effortlessness, he was convinced he could do this all evening and not get bored.

It surprised him to realize he *wanted* to do this all evening. He felt both content and hopeful for the first time in over a year.

A new thought tugged at his conscience. He wasn't looking for romance, but if it found him, would he turn it away? Could he ever find it within himself to trust someone again? To open his heart up to the possibilities?

Meeting Emma had been so unexpected, he wasn't sure what the answers to those questions were, but he would ponder them.

And then a new one formed. If he and Emma were building a friendship, shouldn't he be completely honest with her upfront? Tell her the truth about Willow so she didn't learn it some other way? If he withheld the information from her and she heard about it down the road from someone else, she would understandably be upset.

"Emma," he said, swallowing the uncertainty. "I wasn't completely honest with you before—about Willow."

She paused—only for a moment—but then kept dancing, though her eyes revealed her own uncertainty. "What do you mean?"

"Willow is my daughter." He needed to be okay telling the truth when necessary, so he forged ahead. "But she has a different biological father. My wife became pregnant during an affair."

Emma stopped dancing, and her face drained of all color once again.

Her reaction surprised him, though it shouldn't have. His story was strange, he knew, but he had hoped she would understand.

Emma's heart stopped beating—she was sure of it. She couldn't do anything—couldn't dance, couldn't speak, couldn't breathe.

Willow was Tyler's baby.

"Are you okay?" Clay asked as concern tilted his brow. "You look like you're going to be sick again."

What could she possibly tell him? Shaking her head, she pulled away from his arms and backed into another couple on the dance floor.

"I'm sorry," Emma said as she steadied the woman she'd bumped into.

The lady harrumphed, but the couple kept dancing.

"What's wrong, Emma?" Clay asked as he followed her.

"Nothing—it's nothing." Emma needed to get out of the ballroom. She felt like a fool, running out on him again, but she was afraid she'd tell him the truth if she stayed. And right now she didn't want to tell him anything. She still needed to sort out what this meant.

"It's not nothing," he said. "There's clearly something wrong. Is it something I said?"

"I'm just—It's just—" She was having trouble thinking. "I need to call my sister. I'll see you tomorrow. Good night, Clay."

Emma didn't wait to see if he believed her weak excuse. Embarrassment and devastation warmed her cheeks as she moved through the dance floor, grabbed her purse from their table and crossed the dining room.

She was afraid Clay might follow her, so she glanced back but found him still standing where she'd left him. The look of concern and confusion on his face made her pause—but she had no way of telling him what was wrong. Not yet.

Relief finally flooded her as she stepped out of the lodge and into the cool night air. The sun had set and the brilliant stars blanketed the dark sky. She took a deep, fortifying breath and moved to the side of the deck, out of the light from the windows.

The air was a little chilly and she was wearing a sleeveless dress—but she didn't care. Anything to keep her out of the lodge and give her time and space to think.

How could it be possible that Tyler was still betraying her after his death? She'd thought his damage to her life was done—yet here she stood, learning that he'd fathered a child. Had he known the truth? Had he known he was going to be a father and hadn't told her?

She might never know—but what she did know was devastating enough.

Without giving it another thought, Emma pulled her phone out of her purse and called Carrie.

"Hey!" Carrie said a few seconds later. "Why didn't you answer when I called before? Clay was really worried about you, and I've been worried, too."

Emma took a seat on an Adirondack chair facing the lake. The moon was bright and reflected off the water in waves.

"I'm sorry," Emma said, trying to control the tone of her voice, afraid she'd start to cry. "Carrie—" She paused, not sure how to tell her sister what had happened. Carrie knew everything—well, almost everything.

"What's wrong, Em?" Carrie asked.

"Are you alone?"

"Jack just left to pick up a pizza," she said. "I'm alone for now."

Emma leaned back in the chair and took another deep breath. "This is about Tyler."

"What do you mean?"

"You know he had an affair."

"Of course I do."

"But I never told you the name of the woman he was seeing."

"You didn't think it would matter."

"It does now."

"What do you mean, Em?"

"Her name was Sadie—Sadie Foster."

There was silence on the other end of the phone. Surely, Carrie knew that Sadie Foster was Clay's ex-wife.

"What?" Carrie eventually asked. "You mean Clay's ex-wife, Sadie?"

"Yes."

"How is that possible?"

"They met when Tyler was at a pharmaceutical conference at the hotel she managed. I don't know all the details, but I was able to piece it together when I met Clay today."

"Does he know?"

"I don't know—I don't think so. At least, not that he's told me."

Again, there was silence on Carrie's end of the phone.

"It's worse than that," Emma said, her stomach turning into a knot. She had to stand up and move, or she was afraid the panic would overtake her.

"How could it be worse than that?"

"Willow is Tyler's baby."

This time, the silence on Carrie's end of the phone was deafening.

"It makes sense," Emma continued. "She has his eyes, she's exactly the right age, and Clay admitted to me that Sadie became pregnant while having an affair."

"But he doesn't know that you were married to Tyler?"

"He knows I was married to Tyler—but I don't know if he knows that Tyler was the man Sadie was having an affair with."

"Emma—this is bad. Really bad."

"I know."

"It could ruin my wedding!" Carrie's voice had raised a notch.

Emma briefly closed her eyes as she leaned against the deck railing. She hadn't even thought about the consequences of her sister's wedding—all she'd thought about were the consequences to her life.

"You can't tell him until after the wedding," Carrie said. "I don't want this to hang over everything like a smelly, wet blanket. I want my wedding to be perfect, Em. You can understand that, can't you?"

"I can," Emma agreed, "but I don't want to keep this from Clay, either. He deserves to know the truth."

"He can know," Carrie said, "*after* my wedding is over."

"I'm not sure." Emma paced the deck. "How am I supposed to keep it from him for an entire week? I can barely hold myself together when I'm with him—I don't know what I'll do when I see the baby again."

"You have to keep it to yourself. Please, Em, for my sake. We can sort all this out after the wedding. But for now, please don't say anything. You and Clay have both had really tough years, and you're both starting to come out of mourning. If Clay learns the truth now, it could be devastating for him. He's Jack's best friend, and I need him to be there for Jack this weekend."

"What about me?" Emma didn't want to sound so selfish, but *she'd* been devastated. Why should she carry this on her own?

"We can't help that you know—but if I could, I would have kept it from you until after the wedding, too."

"A small consolation," Emma said under her breath.

"Either way, promise me you won't breathe a word, Em."

Emma let out a sigh. How could she deny her sister this request the week of her wedding? "Okay. I promise."

"Good." Carrie sounded relieved. "You only have five days to keep it together before I get there to help you. Call me if you're feeling overwhelmed, okay?"

"I will."

"I'll be praying for you. I'm sure this won't be easy—and it won't be easy after the wedding, either, when Clay learns the truth."

No. It wouldn't be easy. None of it was easy. But Emma had lived with the heartbreak for over a year and had learned there was nothing easy about being betrayed.

Chapter Four

Clay hadn't slept well the night before, and now, as he sat at breakfast on Sunday morning with Willow, he was tired. He couldn't stop thinking about Emma or her strange behavior the day before. Especially after she'd found out about Sadie's infidelity. Did she really care all that much about Clay's ex-wife?

Part of his heart told him to stay away from Emma. She'd been a wild card all day, her unexpected behavior alarming. But the other part was curious and interested in her. She not only made his pulse strum a little harder, she also seemed genuinely kind and thoughtful. They had so much in common, and he wanted to know more about her.

Besides all that, he was concerned about her health. Was she having some kind of trouble?

He'd seen it all as a doctor. There was nothing she could tell him that would shock him. But he wouldn't press her if she didn't want to share.

His thoughts had gone around and around through the night, and now he was more concerned than ever. He couldn't wait to see her this morning to make sure she was okay.

Clay had ordered scrambled eggs for Willow and had mixed up some of her rice cereal with a little bit of banana puree. She was loving the solid foods he'd been introducing to her, and her appetite seemed insatiable most days. As he fed her, he kept one eye on the steps leading into the dining room. But Emma didn't appear.

"Don't forget," Marilyn Butler said as she walked into the dining room and gained everyone's attention, "there is an ecumenical church service in our forest chapel this morning, directly after breakfast. If you'd like to join us, we'll begin at nine thirty."

Clay had spent the past year struggling with his faith in God. He and Sadie had attended church on and off over the years as their busy schedules would allow. But after she had betrayed him, he hadn't returned to church. He wasn't angry at God—but he didn't know why God had allowed things to play out how they had. Granted, it wasn't God's fault that Sadie had betrayed him—but it felt like God could have stopped it.

Maybe it was time to face his questions head-on and return to church. The forest chapel seemed like a safe place to start—a place where no one would judge him or whisper behind his and Willow's backs.

Clay finished feeding Willow and then ate the rest of his own breakfast.

Emma didn't appear as he cleaned Willow with a warm cloth that Marilyn had provided, and she didn't appear as he left the dining room to follow the signs toward the forest chapel.

He couldn't deny he was disappointed, but he tried not to let it show. He wanted to enter the church service with a clear head and an open heart.

The forest chapel wasn't too far from the lodge, up the hill behind the main building. The path was well marked, and others were on their way to the service. Everyone was quiet and reserved as they entered the place, decorated with a beautiful wooden cross and wooden benches set up under the towering pine trees.

There were several dozen people already seated, facing the cross and Bob Butler, Marilyn's husband, who stood at the front of the group with a Bible in hand.

Emma was there, sitting on one of the benches, her head bowed.

Clay's heart beat a little faster. Should he sit by her? Would she get up and walk away? Or would she welcome his presence? She had appeared to enjoy his company last night, until she'd made a weak excuse and run away from him.

He had to find out, so he walked around the edge of the gathering and over to the bench where Emma was sitting.

She looked up at him, and her expression went from surprise to apprehension to pleasure. But when she looked at Willow in his arms, that same look she'd had when she left the dining room last night returned—a strange expression he couldn't identify.

Why did his daughter make Emma look so uncomfortable?

"Mind if we join you?" Clay asked quietly.

For a split second, she looked like she might tell him to get lost—but then she nodded and moved over to give him space.

Willow was already nodding off to sleep on his shoulder. She usually took a morning nap about this time.

Clay sat and positioned Willow in the crook of his arm. The baby looked out at the others gathered, and her gaze landed on Emma.

Then Willow smiled.

Emma's face softened, and a beautiful smile tilted up her lips.

"I missed you at breakfast," Clay said quietly as they waited for the service to start. "Are you feeling okay?"

Emma took a deep breath and nodded. "I'm feeling just fine."

"You left so quickly last—"

"I'm sorry—I'm usually not so erratic." She smiled again, and Clay believed her. "I'm working through something right now, and I needed to talk to my sister."

He wasn't sure what she was working through, but he, out of anyone, knew how hard it was to grieve. She had lost a spouse to death—something he couldn't even imagine. He should've been the last person to judge her grieving process.

Sunshine filtered through the trees. The air was cooler here in the shadows, but it was so peaceful, Clay felt the warmth of it from his head to his toes.

It didn't hurt that Emma was sitting close to him. Her presence reminded him of the attraction he'd felt for her yesterday. Was it wise to even entertain feelings for someone who was still mourning the death of her husband? They were both so clearly broken.

Clay didn't want to worry or think about things like that right now. He wanted to just be a friend to Emma. To offer her his understanding and companionship. Counting today, they had four full days together before Carrie and Jack arrived. Shouldn't they make the most of it?

"I'm thinking about taking Willow on a hike after the church service," he said, his voice still low. "Would you like to join us?"

"I don't know—"

"You mentioned yesterday that you liked hiking," he said quickly. "I just thought you might want to join us."

She met his gaze, and he saw more apprehension there.

"We wouldn't have to be gone long," he assured her. "Marilyn told me there are some trails crisscrossing the hills around the lodge, and I thought it might be fun to explore them."

He was holding his breath, hoping she'd agree.

Finally, she nodded. "I'd like that."

"Good." He smiled. He'd like that, too.

The beautiful church service lasted for an hour, but Emma could have sat there much longer. She loved the sound of Clay's rich baritone voice by her side as they sang all the old hymns, and she loved the message that Bob Butler delivered from his worn Bible near the foot of the old wooden cross. It was on forgiveness. One of the first messages she'd learned as a child in Sunday school, but one that still resonated now—especially after a lifetime of pain and regret. She had thought she'd forgiven Tyler—but now she realized she needed to forgive him again. It was hard. Especially with Willow sitting beside her.

When the service ended, they returned to the lodge to change for their hike. Emma put on a pair of yoga pants and a tank top and fastened on her hiking boots. The day had grown much warmer, so she filled a water bottle and packed a few granola bars in her backpack to take along in case they got hungry before lunch.

She waited in the lobby for Clay and Willow for fifteen minutes, debating with herself about the wisdom in spending time with the pair. It would be better to hide away in her room for the next four days so she wouldn't accidentally reveal the truth to Clay before the wedding. But she had come to the resort to explore and enjoy, and she couldn't do that from her bedroom.

When Clay and Willow finally appeared, she felt ready to face whatever lay ahead. Someday soon, Clay would know the truth, but Emma would honor her sister and not breathe a word. For now, she'd get to know him and worry about the rest later.

"Sorry we're late," Clay said as he adjusted the baby carrier where Willow was placed, facing forward. She had fallen asleep during the church service, but she was wide-awake now, a happy giggle on her lips when she saw Emma. "She had a major diaper explosion, and I had to give her a quick bath and put her into a clean outfit."

"I guess it's better that she did it while you were in your room instead of on the trail," Emma said with a smile.

Clay made a face. "You're right. But I am sorry. I usually misjudge the amount of time things will take now that I have a child. I used to get out the door in a matter of minutes. Now it takes me four or five times longer."

Emma's admiration for Clay grew by leaps and bounds as she contemplated what he was doing for Willow. This baby was not his biological child, yet he was willingly raising her as his own. Sacrificing his life's plans to care for a baby that had come from his wife's infidelity. The weight of the truth brought tears to Emma's eyes, and she had to look away to cover her emotions. She wanted to believe she could be that selfless, but if the circumstances were reversed, could she raise Willow like Clay was doing?

"I think we're ready," he said, turning to show Emma the backpack he wore. "I have another change of clothes for her, in case the worst happens again."

Willow took that moment to giggle and clap her hands, and Emma couldn't help but giggle, too. The baby was adorable and seemed to be thriving under Clay's care.

Clay opened the front door for Emma, and they left the lodge.

The sun was higher in the sky, and the humidity was rising. Emma had brought mosquito spray, knowing they'd probably need it on the trails, but she left it in her backpack for now and walked beside Clay as they moved toward the entrance to one of the trails.

Laughter from families playing croquet and badminton on the expansive lawn followed them until they entered the woods. Soon the only sounds were their feet crunching along the path, the wind in the trees and the occasional bird calling in the distance.

Emma took a deep, fortifying breath and was happy she had decided to go on the hike.

"Did you get a chance to talk to your sister last night?" Clay asked tentatively as they walked side by side on the wide trail.

Emma looked straight ahead, watching for rocks or tree roots along the path. "I did." But she couldn't tell him what they had discussed.

"I know she was worried about you yesterday." He glanced at Emma. "I was worried, too. You don't have to share anything with me, but if you want to, I'm happy to listen. If it's a medical concern, I could do my best to help."

"I appreciate that." She smiled at him. "But remember, I'm a nurse practitioner. If there was something medically wrong, I would know to get help."

"Touché." He laughed and readjusted Willow's carrier again. "I just want to be helpful."

"I know."

They continued walking, and Emma glanced at Willow, who was starting to nod off. So many emotions tugged at her heart. Betrayal, grief and a deep longing for her own children whom she'd lost to miscarriages. The irony of knowing she and Tyler hadn't been able to create a family but that he had created one with someone else made her chest feel heavy.

"I'm sorry," Clay said quietly.

Emma glanced up at him and found his

dark brown eyes filled with compassion. "For what?"

"You wanted a family, didn't you?"

How could he know just by looking at her?

She nodded and bit her bottom lip for a second to keep it from trembling. "Very much so. How could you tell?"

"Whenever you look at Willow, I can see it in your eyes."

Could he? Did he know what else she thought when she looked at the baby? "Tyler and I tried for years to have one. I had two miscarriages."

"I'm sorry, Emma." The empathy in his voice almost undid her resolve to keep a smile on her face.

"Thank you." She forged ahead. "But I don't want to spend the rest of the week dwelling on all the heartache in our pasts. Tell me something you're looking forward to."

His face brightened and he smiled. He was a handsome man, but more than that, he was kind, thoughtful and selfless. Emma admired all three qualities.

"I'm in the process of selling the home that Sadie and I bought, and I'm looking for a new house for Willow and me to start over in."

"That *is* something to look forward to. Do you have a new house in mind?"

"I've been dragging my feet because I want to stay close to St. Cloud for Sadie's parents—but I also want to make a fresh start and not be reminded of the town where she grew up. I've looked here and there, but I can't settle on a specific house. It's kind of a daunting prospect to know that wherever I choose will become the house Willow remembers from her childhood. It's a big responsibility."

"Timber Falls is only thirty miles away," Emma said before she thought through the statement. What would it be like to have Willow in the same town? To watch the little girl grow up, knowing she was Tyler's daughter? Part of her loved the prospect—but the other dreaded the constant reminders.

"I've only been to Timber Falls once or twice before," Clay said with a contemplative look on his face. "I thought it was a charming town, but at the time, I never thought I'd be looking to move. Are the schools good?"

Emma had opened this particular can of worms, and now she'd have to deal with it. "The school system is great, and my church recently opened up a Christian school that's getting wonderful reviews."

"I'd love to have Willow attend a smaller school, with focused instruction," Clay said, almost to himself. "I think you've sold me on checking it out. After the wedding, I might just have to stop in Timber Falls and take a look around." He smiled at her. "Maybe you'd be willing to be our tour guide."

Her heart did a little flip-flop, thinking about being in Clay's company beyond the wedding. Once he knew the truth about Willow's biological father, would he want to come to Timber Falls? She had the strongest urge to tell him the truth now, but she remembered Carrie's request and her promise to her sister.

"I'd love to," Emma said with a smile. "I think you'll really like Timber Falls."

She had a feeling he would—and she'd like him being there, too, but she wasn't sure if he would want anything to do with her once she told him the truth.

Chapter Five

As they traversed the trails around Lakepoint Lodge, climbing the hillside behind the main building, getting glimpses of the beautiful lake from different lookout spots, Clay began to relax. He found Emma easy to talk to, though he sensed she was holding back bits and pieces of her life—especially where her late husband was concerned. But he didn't blame her. He had no wish to speak about Sadie, either. Better to leave the past where it belonged.

And when he learned that Emma longed for a child and had lost two of them, he understood the look she gave Willow. There was so much vulnerability and pain in her gaze, and he could relate. Not because he had lost a child but because, at its very core, her loss was one of a broken dream—something he had experienced. Even giving up the large Victorian home he and Sadie had planned to remodel together was the loss of a dream.

But today was a new day, and he had a new companion at his side whom he wanted to get to know better.

"Marilyn told me there's a tree house retreat up here that is part of the resort," Clay said as they neared the top of the hill. "She said the occupants checked out this morning and it's being cleaned, but if we wanted to see it, we could."

"A tree house retreat?" Emma asked, keeping up with him over the uneven trail.

"Apparently, it's a tree house you can rent and stay in, like one of the resort's cabins." Clay shrugged. "It sounds kind of cool."

"I'd love to see it."

Willow had fallen asleep with her cheek pressed up against the carrier. She loved to sleep on hikes, and he was relieved, since he hiked as often as he could.

Everything was so quiet and peaceful in the woods, though it was hot and he and Emma were both sweating. The mosquitoes had been a nuisance, too, so they had sprayed their exposed skin and Clay had put some baby-friendly repellent on Willow.

As they got closer to the top of the hill, Clay asked Emma all sorts of questions about Timber Falls. The more she told him, the more he liked the idea of the community. It sounded ideal for raising a family—and at this stage in his life, ideal was exactly what he was looking for.

"The population is just over nine thousand," Emma said, "though a lot of the residential areas outside the city limits make it more like ten to twelve."

"A perfect size. Do you enjoy living there?"

"I love it." When she smiled, her whole face lit up, and he found himself admiring her. The more he got to know her, the less she reminded him of Carrie, though they had some of the same features. Emma was unique and charming in her own special ways.

"You're making me think I'll love it, too," he said, matching her smile with one of his.

She lowered her gaze, and he saw a hint of color rise to her cheeks, leading him to wonder if she was as attracted to him as he was to her. Would she think he was foolish for harboring such thoughts so early in their friendship? Or would she be happy to know he thought she was pretty and engaging?

The tree house came into view, and they both stopped at the clearing to take it in.

They were at the top of the hill and had a magnificent view of Lake Madeline below, with countless trees spreading out all around it. Boats crisscrossed in the water, and a parasailer was flying high overhead in the distance.

"It's magnificent," Emma breathed as she shook her head. "The view is stunning."

"And take a look at that tree house," he said, looking up at the immense structure. A stairway led up to the cabin at the top of the tree. "It's an actual house built in the tree branches."

"Can you imagine the view from up there?" Emma asked.

A golf cart with the Lakepoint Lodge logo was parked at the base of the gigantic tree.

"I wonder if that's the housekeeper's cart," Emma mused.

"Marilyn said if housekeeping is here, we could take a look inside." He nodded toward the building. "Want to see what it's like?"

"Sure."

He loved that she was game for almost anything.

They climbed the stairs and stood on the deck outside the tree house as Clay knocked on the door.

"Come in," called a lady from inside.

"Hello," Clay said as he opened the door. "Marilyn said we could take a look if you were here cleaning."

"You're welcome to look around," the woman said. "We'll be done in a few minutes."

There was a second housekeeper as well, and they went about their business as Clay and Emma stepped into the room.

It was a magnificent space, with windows facing every direction. The bathroom was in the center of the room, but the bed, kitchenette and living space were out in the open.

"Wow," Emma said as she moved to one of the windows facing the lake. "I've never seen anything like this."

"Wouldn't it be incredible to stay here?"

"It would make an ideal honeymoon spot."

"That's exactly what I was thinking. I wonder if Carrie and Jack know about it."

"If they don't, they should seriously consider reserving it for their one-year anniversary."

Clay stood beside Emma as Willow began to move in her carrier, and soon she was kicking her feet and fussing.

"Is she okay?" Emma asked, turning her attention on the baby.

"No doubt she's hungry—and she probably needs her diaper changed." Clay glanced at the ladies who were cleaning the kitchen. "Could I feed and change her here?" he asked one of them. "I have a changing pad in my backpack."

"Sure, honey," the first lady said. "We're due for a break soon, so take your time. We won't need to lock up for a while."

"Thank you."

Clay took his backpack off as Willow began to cry louder.

"Can I help?" Emma asked.

"I'd love that. Can you hold her for me while I get her bottle ready?" The look on Emma's face made Clay stop in his tracks. It was a cross between longing and dread. "Unless you don't want to."

"It's okay. I'd be happy to hold her."

Clay unhooked the carrier and expertly removed Willow. He placed the baby into Emma's arms and watched as her face transformed into pure awe.

Willow stopped crying and looked up at Emma with the same sort of rapture—as if she had known Emma her whole life and had been waiting for this moment.

"Well, hello, sweetie," Emma said as she smiled down at the baby.

If Willow could talk, Clay was sure she would have returned the warm greeting. Instead, she laid her head against Emma's chest and cuddled close.

Emma looked up at Clay with bafflement and surprise written all over her face.

Clay grinned. "She's never taken to anyone like that before," he said. "Especially when she's hungry."

Emma placed her free hand on Willow's back and began to rock the baby.

Clay watched them for a moment, his heart expanding in his chest.

It was beautiful to watch a woman who had longed for a child and a child who would one day long for her mother find one another.

He couldn't stare at them forever, though. No doubt, Willow would soon be crying again, wanting her bottle. Clay worked quickly to prepare it with the supplies he had brought.

The housekeepers glanced at them from time to time, smiles on their faces.

When Clay was done making the bottle, he reached for Willow to take her from Emma. But when he did, the baby started to cry. And this time, she wailed with passion.

"Shh," Clay said, tucking his daughter into the crook of his arm. "Here's your bottle."

He offered it to Willow, but she twisted her head back and forth and refused to take it from him.

"That's weird," Clay said, frowning. "The only time she refuses is when she's not feeling well."

Emma walked over to them and gently laid her hand on Willow's forehead.

Instantly, the baby stopped crying and looked up at Emma.

"She wants her mama," one of the housekeepers said.

"Oh." Emma removed her hand from Willow's forehead and shook her head quickly. "I'm not her mother."

The housekeeper looked embarrassed, and Willow started to cry again.

"Maybe not," said the second lady, "but she wants you all the same."

Emma looked at Clay with a question in her eyes.

"Do you want to try?" he asked.

"Do you really think she wants me?"

"There's only one way to know for sure." He offered Willow to Emma again, and she reached out to take the little girl into her arms.

Instantly, Willow stopped crying.

The look of surprise on Emma's face was

priceless—and made Clay want to laugh. But he didn't think Emma felt like laughing. She wore such a look of wonder that he sobered and handed her the bottle.

Emma positioned Willow in the crook of her arm, like Clay had, and placed the bottle against Willow's lips. She began to suck with gusto—clearly hungry.

"She did want you," Clay said with a smile.

Emma looked up at him. "I wonder why."

"Why?" one of the housekeepers asked. "She loves you."

"But we've only just met," Emma said in astonishment.

"There are no rules about love," said the other housekeeper. "It can happen at first sight—or it can take years to develop. Clearly, the baby loved you at first sight."

Clay couldn't deny what the housekeeper had said as Willow watched Emma. Perhaps his daughter had loved Emma at first sight—and, from the look on Emma's face, he was almost certain that the feeling was mutual.

Before that moment, Clay hadn't been sure that he believed in love at first sight—but as he continued to regard them, seeing it right in front of his eyes, he wondered if he was capable of the same thing.

* * *

The next morning, Emma's eyes slowly opened and she blinked several times as she was pulled from her sleep. Sunshine tinted the eastern sky with vibrant colors of purple, pink and yellow. It should have been peaceful to wake up to such a magnificent view of the lake—but something annoying had brought Emma out of her dreams.

For a minute, she lay there, wondering what had woken her up—and then her cell phone started to ring. When she picked it up, she saw that Carrie had tried calling her a couple minutes ago and was calling again.

Emma blinked away the sleep and pressed the green talk icon.

"Hello?"

"Em, are you awake?"

"I am now." Emma yawned so big, her eyes watered. "It's five fifteen in the morning, Carrie, and I'm on vacation. Why are you calling me so early?"

"I just got the worst email of my life."

Emma sat up, fully awake, her mind racing with possibilities. "Are Mom and Dad okay?"

"They're fine."

"Grammy?"

"She's fine."

"Then what's wrong, Carrie?"

"My cake decorator backed out at the last minute."

Emma leaned against the headboard, relieved that it wasn't a life-and-death situation. "I'd hardly call that the worst email of your life."

"How can you say that?" There were tears in Carrie's voice. "What am I going to do? The wedding is in five days! I can't find a baker so soon. I had to schedule the first one almost a year in advance. This is horrible!"

Emma had suspected her sister would start to panic as the wedding drew closer, and as her matron of honor, it was Emma's job to calm her sister and reassure her. "I'm meeting with Liv Harris today. I'll ask her if she knows anyone who can make a cake for Saturday."

"It will be impossible!"

"Nothing is impossible. It might be hard, but even if we have to buy cupcakes from a local bakery, at least you'll have cake—"

"How could you even suggest something like that?" Carrie was now in a full-blown tantrum. "I won't serve cupcakes at my wedding. I'm going for elegant and timeless."

Emma closed her eyes and took a steadying breath. "I'll ask Liv what she thinks. I'm sure she's dealt with this before. I'm meeting with her around breakfast. I'll let you know what she says."

"Okay—but show her the picture of my dream cake and make sure it's followed perfectly."

"You might have to adjust—"

"I'm only getting married once, Emma. I want everything perfect."

Again, Emma took a deep breath, but this time she had to force herself to bite her tongue.

"Call me as soon as you can. Bye." Carrie hung up the phone.

Emma set her phone on the nightstand and rubbed her face for a few seconds, trying to calm her emotions. A frantic phone call from a stressed-out bride-to-be was never the best way to start the day.

Needing coffee, Emma got out of bed, put on her bathrobe and went into the kitchenette to make a pot of the strong brew. As she waited, her thoughts went to Clay and Willow and the day she had spent with them. After their hike, she had eaten lunch with them and then come back to her suite to read while Willow had taken her afternoon nap. Afterward, Clay had texted her and asked if she'd wanted to go to the beach with them, and they'd spent the remainder of the day playing in the sand and water.

They had eaten supper together, but when Clay had asked her if she'd like to join him after for a hayride, she had declined. It was far too easy to spend time with Clay. And the more time she spent with him, the more she shared and the harder it was to keep the truth from him.

Maybe it would be good to keep her distance today. Focus on the wedding, perhaps take a little nap, finish the book she'd started—anything to keep herself from spending time with him.

After the coffee was done percolating, she took a cup and went out to the balcony to watch the day awaken. A set of chairs faced the lake, so she sat on one of them and closed her eyes to spend a few minutes in prayer and thanksgiving. One of the ways Pastor Jacob had encouraged her to heal was to spend focused time being thankful for her blessings—and there were so many that filled her life.

As she went through the list, she thought again of Clay and Willow.

Could she be thankful for Willow? The baby had accepted her in a way that surprised all of them—but Emma most of all. No matter where they had gone yesterday, Willow had wanted Emma to hold her, play with her, feed her or just talk to her. It was almost as if Willow knew instinctively that she and Emma were connected.

A smile tilted Emma's lips as she felt gratitude for the innocence of Willow's heart. The baby was the byproduct of an affair—something that she had not chosen—and she was just as much a victim as Emma and Clay, perhaps even more so. No matter what, Emma didn't want Willow to grow up with the stigma that she wasn't wanted. And, as much as she could, Emma would see that Willow knew she was a precious gift.

As Emma thanked God for Willow, she allowed the peace of God to fill her heart with the knowledge that this love she had for the little girl was a gift from Him. Emma could have continued to feel resentful and angry about the baby—but in less than twenty-four hours, she'd found a way to be grateful for Willow.

A door opened to Emma's right. She looked toward the sound and found Clay stepping out onto his own balcony, a cup of steaming coffee in his hands. He was also in his bathrobe, his face in need of a shave, his hair tousled by sleep.

"Oh." He stopped. "Sorry—I didn't realize you were out here."

No doubt her hair was just as tousled as his, but when he smiled at her, she wasn't thinking about her hair. All she was thinking was that she liked seeing him first thing in the morning.

"Good morning," she said.

"Good morning."

"Did you sleep okay?"

"Willow was up a couple times through the night. This is the first time she's slept away from home—or, at least, the first time she's attempted to sleep away from home. So I made the coffee extra strong this morning."

Emma smiled, still marveling at his choice to parent Willow alone.

Their balconies were about ten feet apart— far enough away that Emma still felt a modicum of privacy, but close enough for them to speak quietly and not be heard by others.

"The sunrise is gorgeous over the lake," Clay said, took a sip of his coffee and turned to look at the water. "I could get used to this."

"Me, too." Emma didn't live on a lake, but there were several around Timber Falls, and the thought had occurred to her.

"Maybe I need to look for a house on a lake," Clay said.

"That's what I was just thinking."

He smiled as he took another sip of coffee, and she had to look away from him. This pull she felt toward him was getting stronger—and she was now imagining what it would be like to wake up beside him and watch the sunrise every morning together.

It was a dangerous place to let her mind wander.

"Do you have any plans for today?" he asked, his voice quieter than before.

She wondered if he would ask her to spend the day with him again—and though she wanted to, it wasn't a good idea.

"I'm meeting with the wedding planner this morning." She sat up a little straighter. "Then I'm going to work on some of the wedding tasks Carrie gave me."

"If you need any help, let me know. I feel like I haven't been doing much as the best man."

Emma tasted her hot coffee and felt it slide down the back of her throat. It was bitter. "Thanks—but I think I've got it under control."

"Okay." He seemed to pick up on her hint that she wanted to be alone. "Have a good day."

"You, too."

Clay stepped back into his room, and Emma felt bereft for a reason she couldn't identify. She should have taken him up on his offer. Not only were her wedding tasks tedious but she would have liked his company.

Yet—this was for the best. It had to be.

She went into her room and got dressed for the day, taking her time, since she wasn't meeting with Liv until eight. It was an early meeting, but it was the best time for Liv.

When eight o'clock finally rolled around, Emma went downstairs and found Liv sitting in the lobby with a laptop on her knees. She was at least six or seven months pregnant but still looked as stylish as ever. Emma had known Liv since she had moved to Timber Falls and had started attending Timber Falls Community Church. Liv was an interior designer and operated a weddings-and-events business with another woman from church. Her parents had purchased Lakepoint Lodge two years ago, and she had been the one to suggest it as a wedding venue for Carrie and Jack.

"Good morning," Emma said as she caught Liv's eye.

Liv closed her laptop and started to rise, but Emma motioned for her to stay sitting. "Don't get up."

"Thanks." Liv put her hand on her stomach and smiled. "It's getting harder and harder to get up and down."

Emma's heart tightened, wondering if she'd ever know what it felt like to be pregnant for that long—but she pushed aside the thought and tried to think about Liv instead. Or the wedding. Or anything other than her own loss.

"Do you know if it's a boy or a girl?" Emma asked with a smile.

"It's a boy." Liv grinned. "Zane and the girls are thrilled."

Liv and Zane had had a daughter together in high school, and then Zane had gone on to get married and have a second daughter with his wife. After she'd passed away, Zane and Liv had reconnected and started a life together.

"I'm sure everyone will love meeting him," Emma said.

"Especially his grandma and grandpa." Marilyn Butler appeared with a tray full of pastries, bagels and croissants. "Since you two are missing breakfast, I thought I'd bring something for you to snack on. My grandbaby needs all the nourishment he can get." She put her hand on Liv's tummy and rubbed it affectionately. It was apparent by the playful roll of Liv's eyes that her mother did this often.

"I had breakfast before I came, Mom," Liv said.

"Then have a second breakfast—you're too skinny. Isn't she too skinny?" Marilyn asked Emma.

"You don't need to answer that," Liv said as she gave her mom a pointed look.

Marilyn raised her hands. "Fine. I'll keep my opinions to myself."

As Marilyn walked away, Liv sighed. "If only that were true."

Emma bit her upper lip to keep from smiling, but Liv only shook her head.

"Now," Liv said, "what's this about the cake?"

"You heard?"

"Carrie texted me three times this morning."

It was Emma's turn to shake her head. "Do you know of anyone who could whip up the cake of Carrie's dreams with such limited notice?"

"I don't know." Liv put her hand up to her chin as she thought. "I've already called all the bakers I could think of, but none of them are available last minute."

Clay appeared at the bottom of the steps with Willow on his hip. He smiled at Emma, and she returned it.

Liv glanced in his direction, too.

Since Liv would meet him eventually, Emma decided to make the introductions. She motioned for Clay to join them.

"Liv," Emma said, "this is Clay Foster, the best man."

Liv did stand this time and shook Clay's hand. "It's nice to meet you. I didn't know the best man was here, too."

"It's nice to meet you," he said. "It's just a coincidence that Emma and I both came early." He nodded down at Willow. "This is my daughter, Willow."

"Hi, Willow," Liv said as she touched the baby's foot. "You're a cutie."

Clay smiled with pride and then said, "I'm ready and willing to help with the wedding. If there's anything I can do, just let me know."

"Do you know how to bake a cake?" Liv asked, half-teasing.

"Do you need one?" he asked, his face very serious.

"It appears that the cake decorator has backed out last minute," Liv informed him. "And we can't find anyone who is available."

"Do you have a picture of the cake?" Clay asked.

Emma frowned. "Are you serious? Do you know how to bake and decorate a cake?"

Clay nodded, completely confident. "I took a cake-decorating class while I was in med school. I know it sounds silly, but I needed a creative outlet and one of my professors had suggested the class. It turns out that I loved it and—" he grinned "—I'm kind of good at it, too."

Emma and Liv just stared at him.

"You're not kidding?" Liv asked.

"No." He smiled. "Do you have a picture?"

"I do." Emma pulled her phone out of her pocket and tapped on the wedding photo album that she had created for Carrie's wedding. Cautiously optimistic, she showed Clay the three-tiered cake.

He nodded slowly. "That looks pretty doable."

"Truly?" Emma asked.

"Sure. I can go into town and get all the supplies." He looked to Liv. "Do you think I could use the kitchen here?"

"Yes—definitely!" Liv smiled, but she looked a little cautious. "Are you certain you've got this? At the end of the day, I'm the one responsible for making sure everything is done perfectly."

"I'll take full responsibility," Clay assured her. "If Carrie or Jack are upset, you can lay the blame at my feet."

"If you're certain."

"I am—but maybe don't tell her who made it until after the wedding," Clay said. "I'm confident I can pull it off, but she might not be, and I don't want her to worry."

Emma's heart expanded at his thoughtfulness. If Carrie knew they were leaving the cake up to Clay, she would probably have a panic attack. Perhaps it was best if they didn't tell her.

"If you need some help, let me know," Emma said. "I'd be happy to do what I can."

"I'll take you up on it." Clay winked at her and then said, "I should get Willow to breakfast. I'll talk to you two later."

As he walked away, Willow put out her hands and reached for Emma until Clay disappeared down the stairs.

Chapter Six

No matter where Clay went that day, he found himself looking for Emma. Yet he was unsuccessful. After breakfast, he looked for her in the lobby, but she and Liv were done with their meeting. When he went out to the beach with Willow, Emma wasn't there, either. She wasn't in the water, on the lawn or even at lunch.

He tried not to be disappointed, even tried to forget about her. But it was impossible. She was all he could think about. He longed to get to know her better, to see her smile, to hear her laughter. The two days he'd spent in her company had not been enough. He'd never felt like this before, and part of him wanted to spend more time with her just to understand why she affected him this way.

That morning, when he'd found her on the

balcony, enjoying her coffee, his heart had pounded hard. She had looked so pretty with her hair in a messy bun, slippers on her feet and a robe wrapped around her body. There had been something warm and comfortable about her—homelike.

And he wanted more of it.

Now it was suppertime, and he wondered if she'd avoid that, too. Because after a day of not seeing her and knowing she was somewhere at the resort, that was exactly what it felt like she was doing.

As a treat for himself, he had brought Willow to the childcare room so he could enjoy a warm meal. He felt a little guilty as he walked into the dining room without his daughter, but he knew she was having fun with the college-age caregivers who were watching the kids. It was good for both Clay and Willow to have some time apart.

The dining room was dimly lit as families, couples and groups sat around their tables, laughing, visiting and enjoying their vacations. Votive candles added ambience to the space, and bouquets of freshly-cut flowers softened the white tablecloths.

Clay took a deep breath, not wanting to sit by himself but knowing it was his new normal.

He missed Sadie's companionship—though he didn't miss her. He'd been so hurt by her, he was happier knowing she would never be a part of his life again.

But he still didn't like doing life alone.

As he scanned the room, searching for a place to dine, he spotted Emma.

She was sitting at a table for two near a tall window, looking out at the dark evening. Her elbows were on the table, and she was leaning forward, her hands clasped under her chin. She was deep in thought—and he wasn't sure if she'd want to be bothered. But he also knew he couldn't sit across the room from her, knowing they were both alone, without at least asking to join her.

Building up as much courage as he could, he walked across the dining room and approached her table.

She glanced up, and the smile on her pretty face told him she was happy to see him.

His heart beat a little harder, like it had that morning, and he suddenly felt as if this was the first time he'd had a crush. How was it possible that something he'd experienced before could feel brand-new all over again?

"Mind if I join you?" he asked.

Emma shook her head and motioned for him to take the seat across from her.

"Thanks." He sat down and faced her. The candlelight flickered in her brown eyes, and he felt lost for a moment.

"Where's Willow?"

"With childcare. It's nice to have a little break."

She nodded. "How was your day?"

Clay was thankful the server appeared with a glass of water at that moment. It gave him a second to pull himself together—and something to wet his dry throat.

After she took his order, she left, and Clay faced Emma again.

"I had a great day," he said. "I'm happy I had that strong coffee this morning because Willow decided she didn't want to take her morning nap."

"Even though she didn't sleep well last night?"

"I'm beginning to fear that she thinks sleep is overrated."

Emma's smile was so sweet and gentle it tugged at Clay's heart, and he somehow felt like he'd done something important in getting her to smile.

"What about you?" he asked. "How was your day?"

"Good. Thanks again for being willing to help with the cake." She shook her head and frowned. "You weren't teasing us, were you?"

He grinned. "No. I really do know how to bake and decorate a cake. It might not be elaborate, but I think I can make it look like the one Carrie wants. You're going to help me, though, right?"

"Yes—if I can be helpful."

"Do you know how to run a mixer and turn on an oven?"

"Sure."

"Then you'll be helpful. You can come with me the day after tomorrow to get the supplies. I thought it would be fun to take Willow into town. I heard they have a small zoo."

"That would be nice."

"We just need to remember not to mention it to Carrie. A little secret shouldn't hurt her. Hopefully it'll be a fun surprise."

Emma looked down at her glass of water, but instead of smiling, she appeared worried.

"Unless you think she should know," he said quickly.

"No." She shook her head and offered a smile that was clearly meant to assure him, though it didn't. "Carrie has enough on her plate right now. I—I just don't like keeping secrets, though this one is probably a good one to keep."

He wasn't a fan of secrets, either—especially after Sadie's secrets had almost destroyed him. But this one was different. It wasn't meant to hurt Carrie, just give her one less thing to worry about.

They talked about Carrie and Jack's wedding until their food came, and then the conversation turned to Willow again.

"You're a great dad," Emma said as she cut into her chicken. "I really admire you."

Her compliment went right to his heart, and he smiled. "Thanks." He couldn't help but think about her loss and her desire to have children. She was still young, in her late twenties. There was time for her. He wanted to reassure her but didn't know how he could with the feelings that were racing around his heart and mind. He couldn't imagine her having a family with someone else—and that surprised him.

How had his feelings grown for Emma so quickly?

Suddenly, he wanted to know more about Tyler. She hadn't talked about him much, and he knew she was grieving, but he'd often heard that a grieving person wanted to talk about their loved one.

"I'm sure Tyler would have been a good dad, too," he said.

For some reason, it was the wrong thing to say. The second it was out of his mouth, he regretted it.

Emma looked like she was going to be sick again. She started to pull away from the table, as if planning to leave, so Clay reached across and put his hand on hers.

Other than dancing together, it was the first time he had touched her.

She looked up at him in surprise.

"Don't leave," he said, remorse softening his voice. He shouldn't have brought up Tyler if she hadn't first. "I'm sorry."

Emma looked down at his hand.

Instead of pulling away, Clay lifted her hand into his and put his other one on top. "Whatever it is, Emma, you can tell me."

She stared down at their hands for a second, and he was hopeful she'd finally open up to him—but she gently removed her hand and shook her head. "It's nothing."

Frustration mounted in his chest. Something was making her upset, and he wanted her to trust him with it, but she didn't really know him that well yet.

"You can trust me," he said. "I know what

it feels like to be betrayed. I promise you that I would never knowingly hurt someone I care about."

"You care about me?" She looked surprised.

"Of course I do."

"You only just met me."

"Maybe I'm more like Willow than I realized. Sometimes you just know when a person is going to be important in your life. And you're one of those people."

Emma smiled at him—a beautiful, radiant yet shy smile.

The server returned to refill their water glasses and ask if they needed anything. When she walked away, Emma expertly changed the subject.

But as the evening progressed and they talked about dozens of other topics, he noticed that Emma never brought up her late husband. She didn't discuss the life they'd had, how long they'd been married or even how he'd died. Clay sensed there was something deep and painful—beyond the loss of her husband— that troubled her, but she didn't hint at what it might be.

And the more time they spent together, the more he realized that the only way Emma Holt might open her heart to him was if she felt comfortable sharing the truth. It wasn't something he could force—and it wasn't something he would ever pressure her to do. But as soon as she did, he sensed that their relationship would start in earnest.

He just hoped he could convince her he was a safe place to land.

As Emma prepared to leave the resort on Wednesday morning, all she could think about was Clay and Willow. They had spent all day Tuesday together, enjoying the resort amenities, and Emma couldn't remember being so happy.

This morning, they had met for breakfast and then gone back to their rooms to get ready to head into Riverton, the small town near Lakepoint Lodge where they hoped to get all the supplies they needed for the wedding cake. If they couldn't get everything in Riverton, they would go farther south to the next town, which was much larger and would have more options.

They would also take Willow to the small zoo in town, but they wouldn't have a lot of time. Marilyn had said the kitchen would be available to them right after lunch and they could use it until about four, when the cook would need to start preparing supper.

Emma quickly changed her shoes and

grabbed her purse. She was just leaving her room when Clay stepped out of his with Willow in her car seat. He smiled at her in the dim hallway.

"Ready?" he asked.

She nodded and then walked with him down the stairs, through the lobby and out into the warm morning. They'd planned to take Clay's SUV, since the base for Willow's car seat was already secured in the back.

"She'll probably be asleep before we leave the parking lot," Clay said as he finished securing the car seat. "Hopefully she'll sleep while we shop, too."

Emma got into the passenger's seat as Clay got into the driver's seat. She couldn't help but feel like they were a family as they pulled out of the resort and onto the tree-lined country road. This was exactly the kind of picture she had daydreamed about when she and Tyler had been trying to have a family—though it looked and felt much different with Clay at her side.

There was a gentleness to Clay—a quiet strength—that Tyler had lacked. Clay was intelligent, handsome and successful—yet unlike Tyler, he didn't have to prove it to anyone. Tyler had talked about his intelligence and success as a pharmacist to anyone and everyone who would listen. Whether from a lack of his own self-confidence or a need to be recognized as important in his field, he had spent a lot of time talking about himself.

Clay was different. He spoke about his work, but not in a way that brought attention to himself. He didn't mention to anyone that he was a doctor unless they brought it up. His humility about his calling was admirable, and Emma respected him for it.

They discussed the wedding as they drove the ten minutes into Riverton.

"Carrie is anxious to get here tomorrow," Emma said after glancing back to see that Willow was asleep. "I love my sister, but I'm a little worried she's going to be a bit much to handle in the next couple of days."

Clay smiled. "Jack's a little on edge, too. I know he wants Carrie to be happy."

It was Emma's turn to smile. "I've never known anyone who has done a better job. They're perfect together."

"That's what I thought the first time I met her."

Emma loved knowing that she and Clay had a common bond where her sister and his cousin were concerned. It helped her feel a stronger connection to him, though they had only known each other for four days.

She was excited to have her sister at the resort—but she suddenly realized what it meant. It wouldn't just be her, Clay and Willow anymore. After tomorrow, would they even get a chance to be alone again? The wedding would take up all their time, and Carrie would no doubt have a hundred things for Emma to do.

She hated knowing today might be their last time alone together—because after she told Clay the truth about Willow's birth father, she doubted he'd want to spend time with her again.

A pit formed in Emma's stomach, and she tried not to think about Clay's reaction. She hated keeping it from him. Maybe after Carrie arrived, she could talk her sister into letting her tell Clay the truth. He deserved to know, and it was only getting more and more complicated that he didn't.

They finally arrived in Riverton, and Emma forced herself to stop thinking about Carrie and Jack and the conversation she would have with Clay very soon. Instead, she decided that she would focus on today. Enjoy these moments with him and Willow and not let the rest of it cloud her joy in their company.

The first stop they made was the grocery

store. It was small and Emma worried it wouldn't have everything they needed, but they'd give it a try.

"I made a list," Clay said as he secured Willow's car seat into the base of her stroller. The baby was still fast asleep. After he was done, he turned on his phone and showed Emma the list.

It was long and included ingredients for the white cake as well as for the decorations.

"Are you sure she wants a vanilla cake?" he asked.

"Yes. She was adamant about it." Emma nodded. "She wants 'simple and elegant.'"

"I can do simple." He grinned. "Elegant is debatable."

Emma returned his smile.

They walked into the store, and Emma was happy to learn that they carried almost everything they would need. The building was quaint and had a general-store feeling about it, with a lot of gingham and rustic wood. They also carried local products, like honey, preserves and produce.

"They even have an icing kit," Clay said as he stood in the baking aisle. "With a piping bag and several tips to choose from."

Emma smiled at his excitement. "When you

live in a small town, you have to carry everything."

They stood in the baking aisle for almost thirty minutes as they discussed the different options, made decisions and teased each other. Emma could almost forget about everything else as they laughed. Clay's brown eyes were filled with so much light and happiness, she sensed he was thinking the same thing.

When they had made all their selections, they walked to the register to check out. Emma pushed Willow's stroller, and Clay pushed the shopping cart.

"I think we got it all," he said. "I'm kind of surprised."

"Me, too. Now we can take a little more time at the zoo with Willow."

"She'll like that."

Emma wanted to say that she'd like it, too, but she was trying hard to keep her growing feelings for Clay to herself. If she gave in to her heart, it would only hurt worse when he learned the truth.

The lady at the cash register smiled as she scanned each item. She kept glancing at the stroller and then looked from Clay to Emma.

"I think she favors her daddy," the lady said, grinning at Clay. "You two have a beautiful baby."

Emma's cheeks grew warm at the woman's assumption, but Clay didn't correct her, so Emma didn't, either. She just returned the smile.

As they headed outside with their bags, Clay held the door open for Emma and the stroller.

"Sorry I didn't correct her," Clay said. "I thought it would be easier that way."

"It's okay." Emma tried to assure him. "I don't mind."

Affection for Clay and Willow filled Emma's chest—especially when Clay looked at her the way he was right now, as if he didn't mind, either.

As Clay put the groceries into the car, Willow woke up and was ready for a bottle.

"Just a second, sweetheart," Clay said to his daughter. "I'll make your bottle when I'm done here."

"I can make it," Emma volunteered.

"Do you mind?"

She shook her head. She'd watched him make a few bottles the past couple of days and had done enough babysitting over the years to know how to mix it up.

"There's warm water in the thermos," Clay said.

Emma stood near the open door of the car, with Willow in her sight, and prepared the bottle. Willow fussed, but every time Emma spoke to her, she quieted to listen.

Finally, Emma finished and took Willow out of her car seat and walked over to a bench in the shade. She held the baby as she drank, smiling down at her.

Willow looked up at Emma with her brilliant blue eyes, studying her closely.

Clay finished putting away the groceries and returned the shopping cart to the store, then he sat beside Emma on the bench. It was a tight squeeze, but Emma didn't mind that he was pressed against her.

He watched Emma feed Willow for a few minutes before he said, "You'll make a great mom someday, Emma."

His words should have hurt, given her loss, but they didn't. For the first time since Tyler's betrayal, Emma's heart filled with hope at the thought that someday she might be a wife again and a mom. Did that mean she was healing?

How was it possible that it was Willow who was helping her heal? The child who should have made the betrayal feel worse was the very person who was working her way into Emma's heart to mend the brokenness.

Her and Clay.

He put his hand on Willow's leg. His nearness warmed her, especially when his arm brushed hers.

She didn't know how to respond to him—wasn't sure she needed to.

"How is it possible to love someone so much?" Clay asked quietly. "Someone so little, who has done nothing but exist?"

Emma studied Willow's little face, admiring her long eyelashes and the roundness of her cheeks. "It's called unconditional love. It's such a beautiful picture of how God loves us, isn't it? We can do nothing to earn it—yet He lavishes it upon us."

"For a long time after Sadie left, I wondered if God still loved me," Clay said. "I'm starting to realize that His love isn't dependent upon my circumstances or feelings. Whether something is going well or if it's not, He still loves me. Sometimes, He takes things away from us to protect us. In the moment, it feels like He doesn't care, but when we've had time to see the result, it's obvious He cared a great deal."

Emma nodded as he spoke, thinking about how she felt after Tyler had died. She couldn't explain why God had allowed it, and she wasn't about to say that it was for the best—but God had protected her through the storm.

"I have forgiven Sadie," Clay went on, "but I

can now see that God allowed her to leave because it was the best thing for Willow and me."

Emma realized she had forgiven Tyler—but had *she* forgiven Sadie, too? Perhaps the key to complete healing was forgiving the woman who had brought so much pain into her life.

"It's hard to see the good in difficult situations," she agreed. "And sometimes we never see why God chooses to do certain things. But when He does show us, we should be thankful."

"I'm happy He brings people into our lives, too," Clay said quietly.

She finally glanced up at Clay and met his gaze. "Me, too."

She wanted to say more—but for right now, it was enough.

Chapter Seven

Clay was still trying to get his thoughts and feelings under control as Emma finished feeding Willow. He had wanted to put his arms around her, to hold her and tell her he didn't know what was happening to him. But he hadn't. And he wouldn't. It was far too soon, and she didn't trust him yet. She still seemed reserved, though she was beginning to relax more and more with him and Willow.

Emma burped Willow, and the baby giggled, clearly satiated for the moment.

"I think she needs her diaper changed," Emma said.

Clay held out his arms and took Willow. He brought her to the back of the SUV, where he laid out her changing pad.

Soon, he had her changed and back in her stroller.

"Should we stop at the ice cream shop before we go to the zoo?" he asked Emma.

"Sure." Emma smiled and walked beside Clay as they made their way across the street.

The ice cream shop was just as quaint as the grocery store. It had white tables and chairs, with a black-and-white-checkered floor. The smell of freshly baked waffle cones was sweet and warm as they walked into the building.

Willow's eyes were wide as she stared at the tall ceiling and the large cutout ice-cream cone decorations on the wall.

Emma ordered a double scoop of chocolate java chunk ice cream, and Clay ordered praline pecan.

After they got their ice cream, they went back outside and walked to the end of the street where the zoo park and playground had picnic tables. After they finished their treats, they went into the zoo. It wasn't large, but it was well-done and perfect for small children.

There were several families there looking at the bears, the lion and the zebra. Each time Clay stopped the stroller, Emma got down on Willow's level and pointed at the animals. She would name them and talk about their color or tell Willow what sound they made. She was so absorbed in the moment that she didn't seem to notice Clay watching her.

Now more than ever, Clay was aware of what he and Willow were missing in their life. He loved having Emma's companionship. Not only because Emma helped him with Willow but because he loved seeing the world through her eyes. More than once, he'd wanted to take her hand. He had always been affectionate with Sadie and missed that aspect of a relationship as well—the physical touch of knowing someone was close at hand.

Would Emma allow him to hold her hand? Or would she think it was too soon?

When they stopped at the wolf exhibit, Emma stood next to Clay, watching the wolves climbing over their den. He allowed his hand to brush against hers and left it there.

Emma didn't pull away—instead, she used her pinkie finger to brush the edge of his hand—and it sent a thrill up his arm and straight into his heart.

She glanced at him, and he looked back at her, hoping his gaze contained the depths of his admiration for her.

A gentle smile tilted up the corners of her lips, and then she stepped forward to get down on Willow's level to point out the wolves.

Clay's pulse was still thrumming as he squatted next to Willow on the other side of the stroller to watch his daughter's response to the animals.

Willow was staring at the furry creatures, but she wasn't smiling. She looked leery and uncertain.

Emma put her hand on Willow's back, as if she was reassuring the baby.

When one of the wolves jumped off its perch, Willow began to cry, and Emma took her out of the stroller. She put Willow up to her shoulder and walked away from the wolf exhibit, whispering soothing words.

Clay followed with the stroller, admiring Emma's natural grace and her ability to ease Willow's fears.

"You're the only person I know who can get her to calm down so quickly," Clay said. "I might be calling you at three in the morning if she doesn't want to sleep again tonight."

Emma smiled at him over Willow's head. "I wouldn't mind."

As they walked toward the zoo entrance, Clay glanced at his phone. It was eleven thirty.

"If we leave now," he said, "we should get back to the resort around lunchtime. I'll leave

Willow with childcare, and then we can start baking after we eat. Does that sound okay?"

"Will the cake be fresh for the wedding?"

"We'll freeze it until Friday morning, and then we can decorate it that afternoon. It will be nice and fresh for the wedding on Saturday."

"That sounds like a good plan. I don't know how easy it will be to get away from Carrie for a couple of hours on Friday, but I'll try."

"If you can't help me, that's okay."

Emma said, "My parents are coming on Friday morning, so maybe they can help distract her."

They walked along the shaded path, and Emma continued to hold Willow, who was much happier being away from the wolf den.

"Are you close to your parents?" Clay asked Emma after a few minutes.

"I am," she said. "My parents have always been really supportive. They're great at being available when they're needed but awesome at giving us space, too. When I count my blessings, they're always at the top of the list."

"Do you have other siblings besides Carrie?"

"No. It's just the two of us. What about you?"

"I have a sister, but she lives in Ireland with her husband and children. She went there on a mission trip in college and fell in love." He smiled. "We keep in touch with FaceTime and texting."

"And your parents?"

"Two of my best friends."

Emma's smile was warm as she nodded. "I'm happy to hear it."

"They'll be at the wedding this weekend. Jack is their godchild."

When they got back to Clay's SUV, Emma put Willow in her car seat as Clay put the stroller into the back. They were soon on the road toward the resort.

As the day had progressed, Clay became more and more aware of their fleeting time together. Soon Jack and Carrie would arrive and their time would be divided. Then the other guests would come, and he and Emma might not get another moment together until after the wedding was done.

Yet there was time after that, wasn't there? He hoped Emma would allow him to see her once the wedding was over because now that she had entered his life, he didn't want to let her go so easily. And he didn't think Willow would want it, either.

The resort seemed busier than when they had left. Families splashed in the water at the beach, played volleyball in the sand court and enjoyed other activities that were offered. The June weather was near perfection, and it was fun to see so many people taking advantage of the gorgeous day.

"I'll take Willow," Emma offered as she got out of the vehicle. "Do you think you can manage all the groceries?"

"I think so."

Soon he and Emma were on their way into the lodge. She held Willow in her car seat in one hand while carrying the diaper bag in her other. Clay's hands were full of grocery bags.

When Emma pushed open the front door, there was a shriek of excitement and a flurry of activity as a woman rushed toward them.

"Carrie!" Emma said. "What are you doing here?"

Carrie hugged Emma awkwardly, since Emma was holding the baby, and then grinned at Clay. "Surprise! Jack and I decided to come a day early. We didn't want to miss out on the fun you two were having. Oh—look at Willow! She's gotten so big since the last time I saw her. Hi, Clay. It's good to see you again."

Clay tried to hide the grocery bags, but it was impossible. Thankfully, they weren't see-through.

"It looks like you two are having fun," Carrie went on in her excited tone. "Did you go shopping? Is it for the wedding?"

"Yes—but don't look!" Emma moved in front of Clay. "We have a few surprises, too."

Carrie clapped her hands, clearly thrilled and bubbling with energy. Now that Clay saw the sisters standing side by side, he noticed a lot of their similarities—but also their differences. Emma was a few years older than Carrie, but she also seemed a lot more experienced and mature. Emma carried herself with a poise born of heartbreak, while Carrie seemed innocent and naive in a way.

"What do you two have up your sleeves?" Carrie asked. "See, I knew you'd get along." She looked toward the stairs. "I wish Jack were here. He brought our things upstairs. Em, I'm bunking with you until Saturday, right?"

Emma nodded, her back still rigid from the surprise of seeing her sister. "That's the plan."

"Good. Jack will be staying in the honeymoon suite alone until then." She clapped again. "I'm so excited and happy that we're finally here. Jack wasn't sure we should come early, but I convinced him we needed another day to get ready for the wedding. Oh, this is going to be so fun. Do you two have plans this afternoon? I thought we might rent a boat and take it out on the lake."

Emma glanced at Clay, her eyes wide with uncertainty. "Um—we actually do have plans this afternoon."

"What?" Carrie looked between them with dismay. "We came all this way, and you two have plans? You'll just have to cancel them."

"It's part of the surprise," Clay said quickly. "If we cancel our plans, we won't be able to prepare your gift."

Carrie looked from Clay to Emma, then glanced down at the bags, but Clay sidestepped so she couldn't see them.

"Okay," Carrie said, "but I want your undivided attention tonight. Deal?"

Clay tried not to look disappointed—after all, spending time with Jack and Carrie was the whole reason they'd come to the resort. But he had thought he'd have Emma all to himself for the rest of the day.

"We'll do our best," Emma said, glancing at Clay again. "We're going to bring Willow to childcare, and then we're going to eat lunch. Do you and Jack want to join us?"

"Of course!" Carrie gave her sister a side hug. "I'll go tell him you two are back, and we'll meet you in the dining room."

"Sounds good," Emma said.

As Carrie bounded away, Emma turned to Clay. "What are we going to do now?"

"It'll take a little more maneuvering, but we can do it. Let's get everything down to the kitchen before we take Willow to childcare so we don't accidentally bump into them again. We'll go one step at a time from there. At least we can work on it this afternoon."

Emma nodded, but Clay could see that she was a little disappointed, too.

Was it because Carrie had almost discovered their surprise? Or because she was just as upset that her sister and Jack had disrupted their final evening together?

Clay hoped it was the latter.

Emma led the way into the dining room ten minutes later after she and Clay had dropped Willow off at childcare. She was conscious of Clay's presence and had been ever since their hands had touched at the zoo. At first, she had thought the brush of his hand against hers had been an accident, but then he had left it there. Her heart had soared, and she'd hoped and prayed it meant he'd done it on purpose—and, without thinking of the repercussions, she had run her pinky along the edge of his, to let him know she welcomed his touch.

The tension had continued to build between them, and now, as they walked into the dining room to join Carrie and Jack, she felt wound up, about to spring with excitement at the least provocation.

Clay liked her—she was sure of it. And she liked him, too. It was so unexpected and had happened so quickly. Yet there was a lot at stake, and she wasn't sure her tender heart could handle being crushed again. Was it worth the risk?

"There you are!" Carrie said as she waved at Emma and Clay. "We saved two spots for you."

They had found a table for the four of them and were sitting next to each other on one side, leaving the other side open for Emma and Clay.

Lake Madeline and the rest of the resort was easy to see through the large windows and doors. The weather was picture-perfect, and at the moment, Emma wished she was outside instead of in the dining room, about to face her sister. Carrie knew her better than anyone, and it wouldn't take her long to realize that Emma's feelings for Clay had grown quickly.

The trouble was Carrie tended to say whatever came to mind and dealt with the consequences later. If she sensed there was an attraction between Emma and Clay, she would blurt it out, and they'd all be uncomfortable. It would be better to talk to Carrie about it in private, so her sister had time to digest the information. She'd be less likely to say something insensitive if she knew Emma didn't want the world to know. She'd have to try hard not to reveal the truth to her sister while they ate lunch.

"Hey, Emma," Jack said as he rose and gave Emma a hug. "It's good to see you again."

"You, too," Emma said as she returned the hug and then took the seat directly across from Jack, closest to the window. Jack was several years older than Carrie, with light brown hair and blue eyes. Emma hadn't gotten to know him well, but what she knew about him she liked.

"Hey, buddy," Jack said to Clay, shaking his hand and then giving Clay a hug, too. "Looks like you've been working on your tan this week."

"Easy to do when you're at the lake." Clay took the seat across from Carrie. His leg brushed against Emma's as he drew his chair up.

Emma glanced at him, and he looked back at her and smiled.

Her cheeks warmed.

It wasn't going to be as easy to hide her attraction to him as she had hoped.

Thankfully, Carrie seemed too caught up in her own world to notice anything else. She had a dreamy, far-off look in her eyes that told Emma her sister was only thinking about her upcoming wedding.

"This resort is perfect for the wedding, isn't it?" Carrie asked the table at large. "When Jack and I came here to tour it in March, I knew it was going to be ideal, even with all the snow on the ground at the time. But it's even better than I had hoped. Look at that view. And have you seen where the wedding will be held? It's near the lake—far enough away from the beach that we shouldn't be bothered by swimmers, but right by the water. It will be such a beautiful backdrop—don't you think so?"

Emma smiled, Jack put his hand on Carrie's back and grinned, and Clay nodded.

"There's so much to do," Carrie continued. "And I know Liv has assured me that she has the cake under control, but do you know anything about the baker?" This time, she was speaking directly to Emma.

"What do you mean?" Emma asked.

"Do you know who she found to make the cake?"

Emma was stuck. She didn't want to lie to her sister—because she *did* know who was making the cake—but she also didn't want her to worry.

"You need to let some things go," Jack interjected. "If your wedding planner says she has things under control, then trust her and try to relax. That's what we're paying her for. This wedding is supposed to be enjoyable—remember? One of the reasons we decided to get married at a resort was so it could be like a vacation for us and our guests. Everything will be perfect."

Carrie pressed her lips together and tilted her head to look at Jack. Love and admiration radiated from her gaze. "You're right. I love you."

"I love you, too." He leaned over and kissed her.

Emma glanced at Clay, and he looked back at her, his eyes smiling.

She returned his smile, feeling even more connected to him now that Carrie and Jack were with them.

The server took their orders and soon brought them their beverages.

As Carrie continued to talk about the wedding plans, Emma couldn't help but compare Jack and Clay. They were first cousins but looked nothing alike. Clay was tall, with dark hair and eyes, while Jack was medium height, not as trim, and had light hair and blue eyes. Jack owned and operated a land-surveying company and had met Carrie when they'd both played for a winter volleyball league. They had fallen in love quickly and been engaged within a couple months.

When the server brought a basket of bread to the table, both Emma and Clay reached for it at the same time. Their hands collided, and Emma's cheeks warmed again.

"I'm sorry," Emma said.

"No, I'm sorry." Clay tried to hand her the bread.

"You first," she said.

"You first," he countered.

She smiled and took the bread.

Carrie and Jack watched them with curious gazes.

The last thing Emma needed was questions from the engaged couple, so she said to Carrie, "Have you had a chance to talk to Marilyn since you arrived? She's eager to chat with you about the wedding."

Good thing Carrie was easy to distract. She

immediately told them everything she and Marilyn had discussed.

But Jack wasn't so easily deterred, and he continued to watch Emma and Clay with an inquisitive look throughout the meal.

"Do you have plans this afternoon?" Jack asked Clay.

"Um—" Clay glanced at Emma, but then Carrie interrupted.

"I told you they have a surprise they're working on," she said to Jack. "They'll be busy all afternoon, but I made them promise to hang out with us this evening. Marilyn said there's a campfire sing-along tonight, after supper, down by the lake. I thought it would be fun for the four of us to go. What do you guys think?"

"Sounds good to me," Emma quickly said, not wanting Jack to focus on the "surprise" part of Carrie's comments.

"I'd like a chance to talk with you," Jack spoke to Clay, but glanced at Emma. She couldn't be certain, but she thought she saw caution in his gaze. "Would it be possible to borrow you for a bit in the afternoon?"

"Can it wait?" Clay asked. "Emma and I need a few hours to work. But we can talk before supper, if that's okay."

Jack nodded. "Sure. Of course. It can wait."

Was Jack going to warn Clay to stay away from Emma? She couldn't think of a reason why—unless Jack was just concerned for both of them. And rightly so. It was silly for Emma to even consider a relationship with Clay. Jack would realize this, too. There were so many reasons why it wouldn't work—the greatest one being Willow.

"Emma?" Carrie asked.

She looked up, realizing that Carrie had asked her a question. "Yes?"

"I asked if you had a chance to fold the wedding programs yet or work on the place cards."

Guilt weighed her down. "I haven't. Sorry. I was planning to work on it this evening. We've been so busy since we got here."

Carrie lifted an eyebrow, clearly disappointed. "What has kept you so busy? Didn't you come here early to help with the wedding?"

Emma wanted to say that spending time with Clay and Willow had kept her busy—but she wasn't ready to open that discussion at the table.

"I did come to help—but I also came for vacation," Emma finally answered. "This resort has so much to offer. It's kept me busy."

It was the right thing to say. Carrie started to list all the reasons they'd chosen the resort for their wedding as the server arrived with their meals. Emma had ordered the club sandwich, and she enjoyed it as she listened to her sister talk.

Carrie was always one to keep the conversation flowing, and today was no exception. Thankfully, she was so wrapped up in wedding plans, she didn't talk about anything else.

Finally, the meal started to wind down, and Emma became eager to get into the kitchen to start working on the wedding cake.

The server came up to the table and set the check down for them. Clay picked it up, though Jack and Carrie protested.

"Consider it an early wedding gift," he said.

"Thank you," Carrie told him.

"The cook said you can start using the kitchen whenever you're ready," the server said to Clay. "He's prepared a space for you to work."

Emma's heart fell as Clay quickly thanked the server.

"The kitchen?" Carrie asked, frowning. "What do you need the kitchen for?"

Clay glanced at Emma, who was at a loss for words.

"Is that the surprise?" Jack asked. "Are you making us something to eat?"

Carrie continued to frown as she looked at Jack. "Something to eat? We just ate."

"Are you making your homemade pizza?" Jack asked.

"Your homemade pizza?" Carrie looked more confused than ever.

"When Clay asked me if I wanted a bachelor party," Jack explained, "I told him no. But he said he wanted to do something special for me. So I said he could make me some of his pizza. It's the best pizza I've ever had. We used to eat it all the time when we were rooming together. Is that it? Are you making me pizza for supper tonight?"

Clay didn't speak for a moment as he stared at Jack. Surely, he had to recognize that Carrie was already anxious about the wedding— he wouldn't want to add more stress by telling her about the cake.

"Yes," Clay finally said. "I'm planning to make pizza for us tonight. How does that sound?"

Both Carrie's and Jack's eyes lit up.

"That sounds great," Jack said. "It's nice of the resort to let you go to all that trouble. I'll have to thank them."

"No worries," Emma said quickly. "They already know how much we appreciate them."

"Can we help?" Carrie asked.

"No." Clay shook his head. "This is our treat. You two should enjoy a quiet afternoon and let us worry about supper."

Carrie smiled, and then she took Jack's hand. "Let's go down by the lake to see where we'll be getting married."

Jack nodded in agreement, then they left the dining room.

"Pizza?" Emma asked Clay after her sister and fiancé had walked away. "Now we have to make pizza, too?"

Clay groaned. "I guess. I hope Marilyn doesn't mind."

"Where will you get ingredients for pizza?"

"Could you run back into Riverton while I get the cake started? I can make another list."

Emma smiled. "I'd be happy to." She laughed, realizing how silly the situation was. "I hope this is good pizza."

Clay also laughed. "It's the best."

"Good."

"We'd better get busy. It looks like we have our work cut out for us today."

After Clay made a list, Emma headed for the store.

They would have to work fast, or they wouldn't get it all done in time.

Chapter Eight

Clay was in the kitchen twenty minutes later, deep in thought as he ran the mixer. The high-speed whirring noise drowned out all the other sounds of the resort, leaving him to contemplate everything he and Emma had experienced over the past four and a half days.

It seemed impossible that they hadn't known each other that long.

In some ways, he felt like he had known her his whole life. In others, they were practically strangers.

Someone tapped Clay's shoulder and he jumped—but when he turned, instead of finding Emma, Jack was standing there.

Clay turned off the mixer, both surprised and nervous to find his cousin in the kitchen.

"That doesn't look like pizza dough," Jack said, raising an eyebrow at the cake mixture.

"What are you doing in here?" Clay asked, stepping between the mixer and his cousin. "We told you we could handle this."

"When I saw Emma leave, I figured she was going into town to do some shopping—and since you two had just got back from town, you probably hadn't gotten pizza ingredients before." Jack glanced at the mixing bowl. "You're making our cake, aren't you?"

Clay sighed. "Does Carrie know?"

"No. Which is a good thing. She'd freak out if she knew that our wedding cake was in your hands."

"You guessed, though? Before you saw Emma leave?"

"Yeah. I remember when you took that cake-decorating class. I figured it out during lunch—that's why I made the suggestion that you were surprising us with pizza."

"Thanks—I think."

"It seemed like a win-win for me. Carrie doesn't know you're making the cake, and I get my favorite pizza for supper." Jack grinned and leaned up against the kitchen counter as he eyed Clay. "What's going on with you and Emma?"

Clay wasn't prepared for Jack's question—or the change in conversation. He wasn't sure what was going on with him and Emma, and until he knew, he didn't have much to report. Instead, he started to crack the eggs into a smaller mixing bowl. "What kind of question is that?"

"I saw you guys at lunch. I'd have to be blind not to notice that you two are interested in each other."

Was Emma interested in him? He had suspected it at the zoo—but he hadn't let himself think about it too hard.

"Have you told her how you feel?" Jack asked.

"I don't know how I feel." He cracked the next egg and emptied it into the bowl. "I've only known her for less than five days."

"I knew I was going to marry Carrie the day I met her. When you know, you know."

"This is different. Emma and I both had a lot of heartache this past year. I don't even know if she's interested in pursuing a relationship at this point—and, to be honest, I don't know if I'm ready, either."

"Sometimes you don't know until you try." Jack sighed. "I'm aware that Sadie hurt you, but not all women are like her."

"I realize that." Clay frowned. "It's not that I can't trust Emma—" He paused. There was a part of him that wasn't sure if he could ever fully trust someone with his heart again. He knew Emma wasn't Sadie—but how could he be certain that she would remain faithful to him if they started to date or got married?

He didn't.

"How much has Emma told you about Tyler?" Jack asked.

"She told me he died eight months ago—but that's about it." Clay stopped cracking the eggs and studied Jack. "She hasn't said much about him. Why?"

Jack crossed his arms and shook his head. "It wasn't good, Clay. He was having an affair, and she was about to call it quits when they found the cancer. She stuck by his side until the end."

Clay stared at Jack, hurting for her and confused that she hadn't shared the information with him when he had shared his with her. "Why didn't she tell me?"

"I don't know." Jack shrugged. "I'm not sure she would want me talking about him now. I just wanted you to know that Emma understands what you've been through because she's been through it, too. If there's anyone who gets you, it's her—and because she knows the heartbreak of infidelity, I know you can trust her. That's why I told you."

The weight of Emma's heartbreak lay heavy on Clay. He had known she'd been widowed, but he hadn't known she had first dealt with her husband's unfaithfulness. He couldn't imagine the pain she had endured—or was still under. He knew his own pain, but it hadn't been intensified by illness and death. He hurt for Emma, and because he cared for her, he was angry at Tyler, too. The man wasn't here to defend himself—but in Clay's opinion, he didn't deserve to defend himself.

"I just want you to be careful," Jack said. "Not only for yourself, but for Emma, too. She means the world to Carrie, and I don't want to see her get hurt." He clapped Jack on the back. "I'd hate to see you get hurt, too."

"I appreciate that."

"I'm going to meet Carrie at the beach and keep her out of your hair for the rest of the afternoon. I know you and Emma will be busy."

"Thanks."

Jack clapped him on the back again and then left the kitchen.

Clay stood for a long time, staring at the cake batter, thinking about all that Emma had experienced. He couldn't even fathom the pain she must have endured. It was unthinkable.

He slowly added the eggs into the batter and was in the process of pouring it into the prepared cake pans later when Emma walked into the kitchen with a couple grocery bags.

She smiled at him, and he had to force himself to smile back. It was hard to pretend he didn't know the truth about her husband. Especially when it still made him angry.

"Did you find everything on my list?" he asked.

"I think so. That store really does have anything you need." She set the bags on the counter, but she studied him. "Is everything okay?"

Could she see through him so easily? "Jack is on to us."

Emma's mouth slipped open. "Did he tell Carrie?"

"No." Clay shook his head and brought two of the pans over to the industrial-sized oven. "He said he'll keep Carrie occupied while we work—but he figured it out earlier and came in to see if it was true."

"Well," Emma said, shrugging, "we'll do what we can, but if she finds out, she finds out. We'll deal with it when the time comes."

"Or maybe she won't find out." He grabbed

the other two pans and brought them to the oven, then closed the door. After he set the timer, he wiped his hands on a dishcloth and walked around the stainless-steel island to join Emma.

More than anything, he longed to draw her into his arms and comfort her. Take away the grief that was still lingering in the depths of her eyes. Ask her about her heartbreak and relate with her pain. As a healer, it was second nature to him. But he couldn't, not without her wondering what was wrong with him.

He could stand close to her, though, and he did.

They took the ingredients out of the bags, one by one, their hands and arms brushing against each other as they worked. Emma smelled amazing, and the gentle touch of her skin felt good, too.

The awareness between them was still there, creating a tension that reverberated through him. If Jack had noticed it, did Emma feel it, too? Would others see it?

He wanted to ask her if she felt it, but he didn't have the courage—yet.

"We should get the pizza dough mixed up, since it needs to spend some time rising before we put the toppings on," he finally said, his voice low. He'd rather be talking about something other than pizza, but he was happy she was there with him and that they were alone.

"Tell me what to do," she said, her voice low, too.

She rested her hands on the countertop, waiting.

Clay wanted to reach out and take one. He wondered what she would do if he did.

He also wanted to tell her that he knew about Tyler—hoping she'd open up and trust him—but now wasn't the time or the place. He'd rather she tell him without being prompted.

They both stood there for a second, expectation humming between them. Was she waiting for him to make the first move?

A noise broke the moment, and one of the waitstaff entered the kitchen. She glanced at Emma and Clay but didn't comment as she placed a tray onto a pile in the corner and left.

Whatever had been brewing between Emma and Clay was cold now, and he motioned toward the sink. "We'll need to get the dishes cleaned up before we start the pizza. The mixing bowl has cake batter in it, and I'll need the measuring cups and spoons."

"Okay." Emma moved to the sink as she pushed up her sleeves.

If he wasn't mistaken, she let out a small sigh. He let out one, too.

Maybe he would get a chance to talk to her about Tyler tonight, around the campfire. Or maybe he could get her to take a walk with him. Darkness often felt like a safe time to talk about vulnerable issues—when the light of day couldn't reveal more than someone wanted to share.

A couple hours later, Emma turned the key and opened the door into her suite. All the cakes had been baked and were now cooling before Clay would put them into the freezer. The pizza dough was rising, and Clay said he'd bring it to his room. Thankfully, the kitchenette in his suite had a small oven and they could make the pizzas in his room so they wouldn't have to bother the cook again.

Emma looked forward to a quiet supper with Clay, Jack, Carrie and Willow that evening. It would be nice to just sit and relax together.

But for now, Emma had a job to do. She entered her room and went to the container filled with wedding programs and place cards. Both jobs would be time-consuming, though folding the programs might be the easier one to tackle first. She should have gotten it done earlier in the week so it would've been one less thing for Carrie to worry about.

Emma took a seat on the sofa and pulled the programs from the box. She had picked them up from the printer before coming to Lakepoint Lodge and hadn't even looked at them yet. They were simple and elegant, just like everything else. A few well-placed flowers and graceful, black font were set against a white background.

As Emma started to fold, she let her mind wander over her last encounter with Clay in the kitchen. When she had entered, he'd been so deep in thought, he hadn't noticed her at first. She had enjoyed studying him in an unguarded moment. There had been something troubled in his brow, and she'd known instantly that he'd either had bad news or learned something difficult. She hadn't anticipated that Jack had discovered their secret.

But even after Clay had told her what had been troubling him, the concern in his eyes and voice had not abated, and it made her wonder if something else was bothering him. He'd stood so close to her—almost protective, in a way.

She wished she knew what he was thinking or feeling—yet she wasn't in a place to ask him. Until she told him the truth about Willow, there was no way she could speak to him about his thoughts and feelings. Everything was bound to change when he learned about Tyler. It was one of the many reasons she hadn't brought up her late husband. She was afraid if she spoke about him, she'd inadvertently share too much.

The door opened, and Carrie entered the suite with Jack close behind. They were in their swimsuits, and Jack carried a large beach bag.

Emma smiled. "Did you enjoy your afternoon?"

"The sunshine felt amazing," Carrie said. "It's been so long since I've just laid on a sandy beach. It was exactly what I needed."

Jack set down the bag and smiled at his fiancée. "It was something we both needed."

Carrie grinned at him and gave him a kiss. "You're right. We both needed the rest."

They came over to the living area, and Carrie took a seat next to Emma. "Oh! The programs. I haven't seen these since they were printed."

She picked up one and looked it over. "Oh, no!"

"What?" Jack and Emma asked at the same moment.

"I messed up Dad's name!" She let out a frustrated groan. "Instead of *Brian*, I accidentally spelled it as *brain*." She pressed her palm into her forehead. "He's never going to let me live this one down."

"It's a good thing he has a sense of humor." Jack tried to ease Carrie's concern with a chuckle.

But it didn't work. "What are we going to do?"

"There's nothing we can do," Emma said patiently. "These will have to work. There's nowhere close by to reprint them—and most people won't even notice."

"I'll notice—and Dad will notice."

Emma kept folding the programs. "It will be fine. Everyone will understand."

"I guess." Carrie's bottom lip came out in a mock pout. "I read in a bridal magazine that you should expect at least three things to go wrong on your wedding day. I'm counting this as one—and I hope they're wrong. One is enough."

Emma hoped the cake wouldn't be number two.

"Did you and Clay get your surprise taken care of?" Carrie asked as she took a handful of programs to help fold.

"We did." Emma had hoped to get Carrie alone so they could talk about Clay. She had promised Carrie she wouldn't tell Clay about Tyler and Willow, but the longer she waited, the harder it was getting. Clay deserved the truth, and the sooner the better. But with Jack there, it wasn't something they could talk about freely.

They worked for a few minutes, chatting about smaller details of the wedding. Finally, Jack said, "I should probably head back to my room and change. Clay texted earlier and said we're going to eat in his room around six."

"Okay, sweetie," Carrie said as she tilted her head back for a kiss.

When Jack was finally out of the room, Carrie turned back to Emma, her eyes wide. "What's going on with you and Clay?"

Emma opened her mouth to respond that there was nothing going on, when Carrie continued. "It took all of my self-control not to call you two out at lunch today—only because I couldn't be one hundred percent sure that there *was* something there."

"There isn't—not really."

"What does that mean?"

"It means I don't know." Emma scratched her forearm, feeling uncomfortable.

"Do you like him?"

Emma nodded, but she couldn't make the words form. "I know it's happening fast—"

"Fast?" Carrie waved aside the comment. "Look how fast things progressed for Jack and me."

"But you didn't have a late husband who had a baby with Jack's ex-wife."

Carrie's face fell. "Oh. I almost forgot about that."

"I know." Emma put her hands up to her face and groaned. "I need to tell him, Carrie. The longer I wait, the more hurt and upset he'll be. If I had just told him what I suspected from the start, maybe we could have moved on from there. But what will Clay think when he finds out Willow is Tyler's daughter?"

A shocked inhale made them both look up.

Jack was standing at the doorway, his mouth hanging open and his eyes wide.

Dread filled Emma's stomach as Carrie got up and quickly pulled Jack into the room, closing the door behind him.

"What are you doing back here?" Carrie asked. "We thought you left."

"Clearly." Jack looked between Emma and Carrie with shock written all over his face. "What did I just hear you say?"

Carrie glanced at Emma, who swallowed the panic that was threatening to climb up her throat.

There was no use pretending he hadn't heard.

"I think Willow is Tyler's biological daughter."

"That can't be possible—Clay is Willow's

father." Jack had recovered, and his shock had turned to disbelief. "Why would you say something like that?"

Emma didn't want to tell Jack something that Clay wouldn't want her to reveal, but the worst of it was over and she couldn't leave Jack in the dark.

"Clay told me Willow isn't his biological daughter—that she was conceived from an affair Sadie had. And what I know is that the woman Tyler was seeing behind my back was Sadie Foster. So it all makes sense—Willow has to be Tyler's daughter. They have the exact same blue eyes, and she has his nose."

"Clay knows that Willow isn't his?" Jack looked surprised again. "Why hasn't he ever told me?"

"Why should he?" Carrie asked. "He chose to raise Willow as his daughter and probably doesn't want people talking about it behind his back."

"Like we're doing right now." Emma felt ashamed and guilty. "We have to tell him, Carrie. As soon as possible."

Carrie shook her head. "We can't tell him before the wedding. It would complicate everything. It's only a few more days."

"Did you tell Emma not to tell Clay?" Jack asked Carrie.

Carrie nodded.

"That's horrible, Carrie. He needs to know."

"What if he doesn't want to know? Or," she continued, "what if he already knows and it doesn't matter to him?"

"That should be for him to decide." Jack crossed his arms. "I think we should tell him immediately."

"No—please." Carrie pressed her lips together for a second, panic in her eyes. "Not before the wedding. It will put a cloud over everything we've worked so hard for. I want our wedding to be perfect, and if Clay learns the truth, it's going to be awkward and uncomfortable. We don't want that. I promise we'll tell him first thing Sunday morning."

Emma could see that Jack wasn't in the habit of contradicting Carrie—especially where the wedding was concerned. She already knew of several concessions he'd made. But at the moment, she wished he'd stand up to Carrie and support Emma's wish to tell Clay the truth.

"Fine," Jack finally said. "We'll wait—but it has to be first thing Sunday morning, Carrie. I don't want this lingering longer than necessary."

"Thank you." Carrie kissed his cheek. "I promise."

Emma didn't like the plan, but she could hardly contradict her sister's wishes for her wedding, either.

Chapter Nine

The smell of baking pizza filled Clay's suite with savory aromas. Thinking about the fresh basil, bubbling mozzarella and marinara sauce made his mouth water. Even though it hadn't been ideal circumstances, Clay was happy Jack had suggested the pizza. It was nice to have the promise of a quiet meal in his room, away from all the other guests and the loud noises in the dining room.

Willow was wide awake, playing in her activity saucer. Every time she hit one of the buttons, music would play and the lights would flash. She watched it carefully, hitting it over and over, enthralled by the toy.

A timer went off, and Clay grabbed his oven mitts to take the pizza out. He'd made two of them, and the second one was waiting to go into the oven next.

After switching the pizzas, he went into his room and made sure he looked presentable. He'd shaved and showered while Willow had napped, and he put on a little cologne now. He couldn't remember the last time he'd taken such pains with getting dressed. He had always liked to look nice—but over the past six months, he hadn't cared as much.

All of that had changed when he'd met Emma.

He looked forward to another evening in her company. After they finished eating, they'd drop Willow off at childcare and then head out to the campfire.

There was a knock at his door, so Clay called for whoever it was to enter.

When he left his bedroom, he found Jack, Carrie and Emma in the living room. Emma had taken Willow out of her activity saucer and was sitting with her on the couch. Both Emma and Willow were grinning at each other.

Carrie sat next to Emma, tickling and teasing Willow—but Jack stood off to the side, watching. He had a strange expression on his face, though as soon as he saw Clay, he wiped it away and smiled.

"That pizza smells amazing," Carrie said. "I could smell it out in the hallway."

Emma glanced up at Clay and offered him a gentle smile. He returned it.

"It looks like it turned out well," Jack said as he walked into the kitchenette and looked at the pizza cooling on the counter.

"The second pizza should be ready in about ten minutes," Clay said, "but we can cut into this one."

He had thought ahead to ask the kitchen if he could borrow a pizza cutter, since there was none in his little kitchenette. As Emma and Carrie entertained Willow, Clay cut the pizza and Jack got the plates and napkins set out on the counter.

Willow started fussing for something to eat, so Clay pulled her portable high chair out of the corner and brought it into the living room.

Emma set her into it and strapped the harness to hold her in place. Clay secured the tray, and Emma grabbed the bib off the counter. She put it on Willow while Clay peeled a banana and cut it into small chunks on the high chair tray.

"Wow," Carrie said as she rose to get a piece of pizza. "You two look like you've been doing that together for years."

Clay smiled at Emma. He loved how easily they worked together and how she seemed to know exactly what Willow needed.

Though Carrie was also smiling, Jack wasn't. He watched all of them with a strange expression on his face, as if he was both curious and troubled at the same time.

"You okay, Jack?" Clay asked.

Jack startled, and his face cleared as he nodded. "Yep. Everything's good."

Emma glanced at Jack, her own concern tightening her brow for a second.

But it was Carrie, who frowned at Jack and shook her head, that made Clay wonder.

"Something going on?" Clay asked.

Carrie grinned and shook her head.

Clay decided to put it out of his mind, chalking it up to something, probably wedding-related, that Carrie and Jack were working through. It wasn't Clay's business, unless Jack asked him for advice.

Everyone filled their plates and sat around the living room to eat and visit.

Emma sat on one side of Willow's high chair, and Clay sat on the other. As soon as she finished her bananas, Clay was ready with puffed rice cereal.

The entire time they ate, Clay kept getting this strange feeling that something was off with Jack. Whether it was the way he watched Willow out of the corner of his eye or how quiet he was as they all visited or that he just seemed different, Clay was starting to get worried. Jack was usually the life of the party. He liked to laugh, tell jokes and relive old memories through his stories. But tonight, he just ate his food and observed the rest of them.

Now Clay not only wanted to talk to Emma about her late husband but he was going to have to figure out what was wrong with Jack. He hoped he wasn't getting cold feet or had changed his mind entirely about marrying Carrie.

When they were done eating, Clay grabbed a dish towel from the kitchenette and cleaned Willow's hands and face while Emma grabbed her high chair tray and ran it under the sink.

Clay took Willow into the bedroom to change her diaper and put her into pajamas, and when he came back into the main living area, only Emma remained in the kitchenette. She had cleaned the space and was just putting the leftover pizza in the refrigerator.

"Carrie and Jack said they'd meet us by the campfire," Emma said.

"Thanks for cleaning up."

"Thanks for making supper."

Willow reached for Emma, and she took her,

so Clay let her go. His heart expanded every time Willow and Emma interacted.

"Ready?" Emma asked him.

Clay nodded and picked up Willow's diaper bag to bring to the childcare room.

They left Clay's suite, and Emma stopped at hers to grab a cardigan, then they walked downstairs to drop Willow off.

When Emma put Willow into the caregiver's arms, Willow began to cry and reach for Emma again.

The look on Emma's face was both heartbreaking and priceless.

"She wants me?" Emma asked.

"We'll take good care of her," the caregiver said. "A lot of babies cry when their mamas drop them off. You don't need to worry."

Emma's face said otherwise as she looked at Clay. "Maybe we shouldn't leave her."

"It's okay, Emma," he assured her. "We're not leaving the resort. If they need us, they have my cellphone number and we can be back here in minutes."

She didn't look so sure, so he took her hand in his, said good night to Willow and then led Emma out of the room.

Emma's hand felt so small and delicate in

his own, and when she entwined her fingers through his, his heart raced.

"Are you sure she's okay?" Emma asked quietly in the dim hallway.

Clay looked down at her and had the urge to promise her that it would all be okay—as far as it depended on him anyway. Not only with Willow, in this moment, but into the future as well.

"She'll be fine," he said, tightening his hold on her hand ever so gently.

She looked down at their hands—but she didn't pull hers away, and neither did he.

"Clay—" She broke off.

He couldn't see her eyes and suddenly realized how much he enjoyed looking into the depths of them, to see her feelings and emotions playing about in her expressive gaze.

When she didn't continue, he pulled her a little closer. "What is it, Emma?"

She finally looked up at him—but then she shook her head and pulled back, untangling their hands. "Nothing." She forced a smile. "Let's go and see if Carrie and Jack are at the campfire."

Emma turned and led the way toward the lobby.

He wished he knew what she had wanted to

say. He also wanted to ask her about Tyler—but he would wait until they had more privacy and time to talk.

Emma hadn't been prepared for the moment in the hallway with Clay. He'd held her hand so gently, yet with such confidence, that she had been almost speechless. She had wanted to tell him the truth about Tyler and Willow, but then she'd remembered the promise she had made to Carrie and kept the information to herself.

Had Clay taken her hand on instinct, to reassure her as they'd left Willow in tears—or had he taken her hand because he had been looking for a reason to do just that?

Now, as they walked out of the lodge and into the cool evening, she wondered if he'd try to take her hand again. More than anything, she longed for him to hold her—but each time she thought about Tyler and Willow, she felt herself pulling away, both physically and emotionally. The dread of him finding out the truth was starting to make her feel ill.

"Carrie said the campfire was going to be near the beach," Emma said, wanting to fill the silence between them.

They walked side by side on the path leading to the lake. The sun was just setting in the west, behind the lodge, casting brilliant rays of purple, pink, orange and yellow across the sky. It bounced off the clouds, splaying out in several different directions.

Clay put his hands into his pockets and became pensive.

At least he wasn't going to reach for her hand again.

"I don't like to pry," Clay said cautiously, "but are Jack and Carrie doing okay? He seemed a little off this evening. I hope they're not fighting."

Emma briefly closed her eyes and then turned to look toward the line of trees to her right. She had noticed Jack's odd behavior, too, and knew it was because he was aware of Willow's connection to Tyler. She had hoped that Clay wouldn't notice, but she should have known better. One of the reasons she liked him was his perceptiveness.

"I think they're doing great." She didn't know what else to say.

"Didn't you think he was acting a little strange at supper?"

"Um…" Emma continued to look away from Clay. "I'm not sure." She wished Carrie would just let her get this over with.

"Maybe I can find some time to talk to him

tomorrow. See if something is bothering him. I've known Jack his whole life, and he hasn't been able to keep things from me for long. If there's trouble, he'll share."

What if he did share? What if he told Clay the truth? Emma was the one who needed to tell Clay about Willow. If it came from someone else, he'd be even more hurt.

She didn't know what to say, so she said nothing. She'd need to warn Carrie and Jack that Clay was going to try to get the truth out of him—and then maybe Carrie would finally let her say something.

There were at least a dozen people already around the campfire when they joined the group. Logs had been turned onto their sides for seating, and a gentleman with a cowboy hat was strumming familiar songs on his guitar. There were children as young as five or six roasting marshmallows over the flames and adults as old as eighty sitting around watching them with smiles on their faces. Everyone in between was scattered around the perimeter of the fire. Some were singing, while others were just enjoying the sound.

Carrie and Jack were there, sitting arm in arm. Carrie motioned for Emma and Clay to join them. There wasn't much room on the log, so they had to sit close.

Emma sat first, and then Clay pressed in beside her. It was warm, between her cardigan, the fire and his presence. But she didn't mind. She loved being close to him. It was a feeling she could get used to—one she was starting to crave.

"Are you comfortable?" he asked, for her ears alone.

She nodded and smiled, loving the way he looked at her.

They soon joined in the singing. Clay's voice was strong and melodic, just as it had been at the church service in the woods. She wouldn't have been surprised if he had been in a choir or had lessons at some point in his life. His pitch was perfect as his voice rose above the others. Several people even turned to look in his direction, smiling at his contributions to the popular songs.

The water lapped against the shoreline behind them, and the fire continued to crackle as the evening wore on. One of the little girls offered Emma a roasting stick, so she roasted some marshmallows and enjoyed a s'more. She made one for Clay and Jack, but Carrie declined, making a half joke about not wanting to risk not fitting into her wedding gown.

Soon, the stars were sparkling overhead and people began to wander away from the campfire, thanking the guitarist.

"I think we'll head in," Carrie said as she and Jack rose from their bench. "We're going to rent a speedboat tomorrow and go waterskiing, if you guys want to join us."

Emma and Clay looked at one another as if to gauge the other's interest, and she realized she hadn't done that with anyone since she'd been married to Tyler.

Her cheeks warmed, and he glanced down for a second.

"I'd love to go out on a speedboat," Emma said.

"Same here," Clay added. "I'll sign Willow up for childcare again."

"Okay. Let's plan to take a picnic lunch out on the lake." Carrie seemed excited about the possibility. "We'll discuss it more at breakfast. 'Night, you two. Don't stay up too late."

"Good night," Emma and Clay echoed.

Emma wasn't ready to head in for the evening. She didn't think she'd be able to sleep, even if she tried. Her heart and mind were so full of thoughts of Clay.

Clay didn't seem interested in going in, either. They stayed close to each other on the log, even though Carrie and Jack had left.

After a couple minutes, Clay tilted his head toward Emma. "Want to take a walk?"

Her insides filled with butterflies at his request. It was one thing to be with him during the day or to have Willow or her sister and Jack with them. It was another entirely to walk alone with him at night. The more time she spent with him, the clearer it was that she liked him— more than she wanted to admit to herself. She shouldn't say yes, shouldn't encourage this to continue with everything that was still unsaid. And even if everything was out in the open between them, she wasn't sure if her heart was ready. It had been so bruised and battered, she didn't know if it would ever heal.

Yet—she wanted to walk alone with him. Wanted to explore the possibilities and feel *something* again. Clay was different from Tyler in every single way. Did that mean she could trust him? Trust herself *with* him? She wanted to find out, and the only way to do that was to try.

"Okay," she said quietly.

Clay stood and offered his hand to her. She took it and he helped her stand, but he didn't let it go as they moved around the fire and toward the lake walk.

His hand was warm and gentle, reminding her that he was a doctor. She could picture him at work. He was sure to be patient and kind, his hands tender as he healed. He had a calling in his life to heal, just as she did. It was one more reason she liked him.

"Do you mind if I hold your hand, Emma?" Clay asked as they moved farther away from the campfire. The sounds of the music faded as the night closed in around them, cocooning them in privacy. A loon called from the lake, and the whisper of a soothing wind echoed in the trees.

"No," she said truthfully, though her heart was pounding so hard, she wondered how she had managed to say the simple word.

He ran his thumb over the top of her hand, causing goose bumps to rise on her arms. "Good," he said.

They walked alongside the lake, passing all the waterfront cabins. Lights were glowing from within, but their path was dark. Emma's eyes had adjusted enough that she could see the boardwalk in front of her.

Neither spoke for a few moments, though Emma had so many things she wanted to say.

It was Clay who finally broke the silence. "I know we just met, but I really like you, Emma, and I don't think I'm hiding it well."

She could hear the smile in his voice.

"I hope we'll be able to see each other after the wedding," he continued.

She inhaled, getting a whiff of the heady cologne he was wearing. She felt adrift at the newness of these feelings for a man she hardly knew—yet one who was so intertwined with her life, it was frightening. She wanted to see him again, too, but she had to tell him about Tyler—at least, about his infidelity, so that when he learned the rest, it wouldn't be such a blow.

"I hope we can see each other, too," she said.

He drew her a little closer, and she knew she needed to stop the trajectory of his thoughts. She couldn't encourage him—not yet.

"I haven't told you about Tyler." It was blunt and a bit jarring, but she didn't know how else to bring up the topic.

"I had hoped you would tell me." His voice was still low. "I hope you can trust me with your past, Emma."

She briefly closed her eyes. The word *trust* had come to mean so much more to her because she had lost it. She struggled to trust anyone in her life—even her sister, whom she loved dearly. It hurt to trust people. To lay her heart at their feet and hope they would be gentle with her. But if she couldn't trust, then what hope did she have to love again? The two went hand in hand.

"You know Tyler died." She paused and swallowed the emotions trying to overcome her. "What I haven't told you is that he cheated on me, too, and we were separated when he was diagnosed with cancer."

Clay came to a stop at the end of the line of cabins. There was a lookout at the lake, framed perfectly by trees. When he turned to face her, his back to the lake, she could see his face from the glow of lights in the last cabin.

"I'm sorry, Emma. More than you know."

She nodded. "I know you understand."

"Only to a point. Sadie cheated—but she didn't die. I can't imagine how difficult it was for you to watch Tyler struggle, on top of everything else."

"It was the hardest thing I've ever done—and that's why I need to be careful. My heart is still so tender and raw." She paused before she said, "I'm afraid."

He was still holding her hand, so he took the other. "I'm afraid, too, Emma."

She believed him. If there was anyone in the world who could relate to her, it was him. Her affection for him grew by leaps and bounds, scaring her with its intensity.

Slowly, Clay lifted one of his hands and touched Emma's cool cheek.

Her breathing became shallow as she looked into his eyes, wondering what it would feel like to be loved and cherished by Clay Foster. Somehow, she believed their brokenness would fit together and they might become whole—but as he bent toward her, and she was certain he would kiss her, she became rigid and felt herself pulling away.

She couldn't let him kiss her—couldn't let him trust her, not when she had a secret that would tear at his heart, just as it had hers.

He paused, a question in his beautiful gaze. "Emma?"

"I can't," she whispered. "I'm sorry."

She pulled away even more, taking her hand out of his. She shouldn't have let it go this far. She shouldn't have come with him and put them both in this position. There was a part of her that had known what was happening—but she wouldn't be able to forgive herself if she hurt him more.

Tomorrow was Thursday. She only needed

to wait three more days before she could tell him the truth about Willow. Surely, if this was real and he cared about her, three more days wouldn't matter.

But it wasn't just that. She needed to tell him everything before she let him kiss her—or she'd regret it for the rest of her life.

Clay didn't ask any more questions as they walked back to the lodge together.

And he didn't try to take her hand again.

Chapter Ten

Emma's heart was still pounding as she left Clay in the lobby. All she wanted to do was get away to her room and be by herself. But she needed to find Carrie and Jack and tell them that Clay was planning to talk to Jack about what was bothering him.

As she walked up the stairs, Emma texted Carrie and asked where she and Jack had gone.

The reply from Carrie was almost immediate. She told Emma they were in her suite.

Emma put her phone away and was soon at her room. The door was unlocked, so she entered and found Carrie and Jack on the couch, cuddled up under a blanket, watching a black-and-white movie on the television.

Carrie glanced up at Emma and smiled. "You're back early."

"Can I talk to you two?" Emma asked.

"Sure." Carrie paused the television and sat up straighter.

Jack looked like he had fallen asleep but was blinking himself awake as he looked toward Emma.

She took a seat on the only other chair in the living room and faced them.

"Clay knows something is bothering you, Jack."

"I told you he suspected something," Carrie said. "You're not very good at keeping secrets."

"Which is something you should admire about me," Jack said, sitting up. "I hate keeping things from people. I have a horrible poker face."

"This is important," Carrie countered. "Clay can't know anything about Willow until Sunday."

"He said he was going to talk to you about it," Emma told Jack.

"Another reason I think we should tell him." Jack turned back to Carrie. "This is ridiculous."

"Do you think he'll get upset?" Carrie asked.

"Yes—I think he'll be extremely upset."

"Then I don't want him to know." Carrie stood, and the blanket they'd been using fell to the floor. "This is my wedding, Jack, and I want everything to be perfect."

"Why does this matter so much to you?" Jack asked.

Tears came to Carrie's eyes. "Because everything has been about Emma all year. For once, I want things to be about me."

Emma's mouth slipped open as Carrie turned to her. She'd had no idea her sister felt this way.

"None of it was your fault," Carrie said, "but it *has* been all about you and Tyler this year. I thought that *finally* the attention would be off you for a few days and people would look at me. But then this happened, and it's threatening to be all about you again."

Pain and anger sliced through Emma as she stood to face her sister. "I wouldn't have wished for any of the attention, Carrie. It's been the worst year of my life. I'd trade it for almost anything."

Carrie dashed away her tears. "I know—I'm not blaming you. I just want things to be normal for a few days. I want to be happy—to celebrate something good instead of mourn and be upset about something bad. Can you two understand that?" She looked between Emma and Jack. "Just give me a few more days. Please.

It's all I'm asking. And then I'll let the whole thing blow up."

Jack nodded, and Emma looked down at her hands, unable to meet her sister's gaze. Her words hurt because they were true—but also because it wasn't Emma's fault. The circumstance that had led to all the attention had been horrific. To know that Carrie was upset with her for something she hadn't caused felt like salt on a festering wound.

Emma turned and walked toward her bedroom.

"Em—"

"No." Emma shook her head. "I need some space, Carrie."

She closed the door and leaned against it.

Tears trailed down her cheeks and dripped off her chin. She understood her sister's desire for a little normalcy, and she would honor her wish, though she knew it would come at a great cost. Would Clay ever forgive her for not telling him the truth right away? And how could Emma convey to Carrie her fears that this might destroy the one good thing that had happened to her all year?

She couldn't—and she wouldn't even try. This was Carrie's wedding, and it would be all about Carrie this weekend. No matter what it might cost Emma.

She sat in the rocking chair near the window and pulled out her phone. She hadn't been able to look at her old pictures in a long time—not since Tyler had died. It had been too painful to see the memories that should have been happy but were tainted by everything that had happened. They had gone to Hawaii just a couple months before Emma had learned about Tyler's affair. He'd already been in the midst of it while they'd been there, though she hadn't known about it. Everything after that day felt like it had been stained.

She opened the photo app on her phone and took a deep breath as the tears continued to fall. She wasn't sure what she hoped would happen when she saw them, but she needed to face her past.

Face Tyler.

As soon as the pictures from Hawaii appeared, the memories came flooding back. Snorkeling in Hanauma Bay, hiking up Diamond Head, learning to surf near Waikiki Beach, visiting Pearl Harbor. The trip had been amazing.

The truth was, there had been good times. She and Tyler had been happy before the miscarriages and the infidelity. And despite his betrayal, he had loved her. None of that was a lie.

As she scrolled through the pictures, she suddenly stopped to stare at a snapshot of Tyler. He was sitting on Kawailoa Beach, near Haleiwa, playing a ukulele he had just purchased. She had called his name, and he had looked up at her. His blue eyes were so vibrant in the picture, reminding her of Willow.

Sweet, innocent, lovable Willow. Just thinking about the little girl brought such joy and peace to Emma's heart. Perhaps it was because a small part of Tyler was still with her in Willow—or because Willow seemed to love her unconditionally. She didn't know which. Whatever it was, seeing Tyler, remembering the good times they'd had didn't hurt like it had before.

It suddenly dawned on Emma that if Tyler hadn't cheated on her with Sadie, Willow wouldn't exist. Emma didn't celebrate Tyler's affair—but she could see the beauty that had come from the ashes of the pain. It was just like God to create a priceless gift out of the wreckage.

And if He could do that with something as devastating as an affair, what else could He do with the brokenness of Emma's life?

She turned off her phone and closed her eyes. Her tears of pain had subsided, and tears of thanksgiving replaced them. She quietly thanked God for allowing her to see the blessings that had been brought into her life through Clay and Willow and asked Him to help her be patient as she waited for the wedding to come to an end.

She also made the decision to forgive Sadie for her part in Emma's pain. If Clay could forgive her, then Emma could, too. It didn't take away the scars, but it helped them to heal.

More now than ever, she wanted Clay to know the truth, and to see what would come of it. Would he be unable to forgive her? Would he lose what little trust he might have for her?

She didn't know—but she had to believe that God had a bigger plan than hers and that His plan would ultimately bring about the best outcome for all of them.

Even if it meant she and Clay had to go their separate ways.

"Em?" Carrie knocked on the door. "Can I come in?"

Emma wasn't sure she was ready to talk to her sister, but she knew Carrie didn't like things to sit and fester for too long.

"Sure," Emma called.

Carrie slowly opened the door and entered the dark room. She walked over to Emma and knelt by her. "I'm sorry."

"I know. I'm sorry, too."

"You don't have anything to be sorry about." Carrie put her hand on Emma's knee. "I know I'm being selfish."

"You're not selfish, Care. You're just tired and heartsore, like the rest of us. And you want to move on and start celebrating some of life's happier moments." Emma smiled. "It's your wedding. You should be able to enjoy it to the fullest."

"But not at the expense of hurting my big sister."

"I'm going to be okay."

"I know you are." Carrie squeezed Emma's knee. "And I know things will work out with Clay. I see you two together. It's like you were made to be a team. I don't even think you two realize how well you work and move together. It's like you've known each other your whole lives. It's pretty incredible to see."

Emma wished she shared her sister's confidence. She wasn't sure that things would work out with Clay, and the longer she waited to tell him about Willow, the more she feared it was all coming to an end.

* * *

Clay didn't go to breakfast the next morning, and he wasn't even sure if he should join the others on the speedboat that afternoon. If he hadn't already committed to going and signed Willow up for childcare he might have skipped.

It wasn't because he didn't want to see Emma—the opposite was true. All he wanted was to be with her. But last night, when she had pulled away from him, moments before he'd hoped to kiss her, he'd realized how dangerously close he'd come to falling in love again.

And he couldn't fall in love. It hurt too much to risk his heart, especially when he had Willow to think about now. He'd hardly survived the loss of his marriage, and Willow hadn't been aware of losing Sadie.

But now, as Willow was getting older and already bonding with Emma, he couldn't risk hurting her, too.

It would be better to avoid Emma for the rest of the week and put some distance between them. But that was impossible, since the next few days were going to be all about the wedding. As the best man and matron of honor, they were bound to be together a lot.

Which meant he only had one choice: ignore his growing feelings for Emma. Which sounded easier said than done when he could hardly think about anything other than her.

He left Willow at childcare and walked toward the lake. He was early, but he hoped to have a few minutes to himself before the others joined him. It would take a lot to ignore his feelings for Emma, but he could do it. He had to do it.

A dock was set up near the cabins where Clay had almost kissed Emma last night. As he walked past the lookout where they had stood, he forced himself not to think about what had happened. He was already on edge, afraid it would be weird with Emma when he saw her today. He was slightly embarrassed that he had even tried kissing her. If she hadn't stopped it, he was certain he would have lost his heart to her.

He was happy she had pulled away—but the only trouble was now that he'd been so close to kissing her, he wanted it even more than before.

Jack was loading things into a red speedboat when Clay approached.

"Hey," Clay called out to him as he walked down the metal dock. "Need help?"

"Sure." Jack motioned to the cooler on the dock. "You're just in time to help me with lunch."

The cooler was heavier than Clay had expected, and it took the two of them to hoist it into the back of the boat.

"What's in here?" Clay asked.

"It's mostly filled with ice, but Carrie had the cook prepare lunch and there's way more food in there than the four of us can eat."

"Where are Carrie and Emma?" He glanced toward the shore.

"They're coming. The wedding planner stopped in to talk to them after breakfast, and it's taking longer than expected." Jack finished storing the beach towels and stood up straight. "Where were you this morning? We thought you'd join us for breakfast."

Clay looked toward the lake, trying not to let his emotions show on his face, though he knew it was no use. He and Jack had been through a lot together, and he trusted him more than anyone.

"Things got a little awkward between Emma and me last night."

"Ah." Jack nodded and crossed his arms.

"Did she mention anything?"

"No."

"Right. I don't know why she would. Nothing really happened."

"Did you want something to happen?"

Clay ran his hand through his hair in frustration. "I almost kissed her."

Jack's eyebrows jumped. "What?"

"She stopped me." Clay shook his head. "It's probably better that way. Things are still complicated from my divorce."

"Your divorce was finalized, right?"

"Of course."

"Then what's so complicated?"

"Everything. I'm raising a baby, trying to establish my medical practice and looking for a new home where Willow and I can make a fresh start." He remembered his conversation with Emma about Timber Falls, but he wasn't sure that was such a good idea anymore. "Every time I think I know what I want, I change my mind."

"You know what you want, Clay. You want what most of us want—what you thought you already had with Sadie. A happy marriage, healthy children, a successful career and a comfortable home. It's not that complicated."

Clay sighed. "When you say it like that, I guess you're right."

"You've got a healthy kid, your career is taking off and you're on your way to a comfortable home. All you need is the happy marriage." Jack studied Clay. "And I think you know that

Emma is exactly what you're looking for, and that's what scares you more than anything. Until now, you didn't think you'd find anyone like her. But now that you have, it's time to decide if you're ready to put yourself out there again, and that's scary."

He was right. Clay was afraid—just like Emma was afraid. It was probably why she had pulled away last night.

"At some point," Jack continued, "you're going to have to face your fear and make a decision. If you wait too long, Emma might not be there when you get around to it."

Clay nodded, though he had a lot to think about—and he wasn't sure he wanted to do it right here. Choosing to pursue a romantic relationship wasn't a decision he could make standing in a boat with his cousin.

"Are you and Carrie doing okay?" he asked Jack, wanting to change the subject.

"Yeah, why?"

"You seemed off yesterday."

Jack didn't meet Clay's gaze as he absentmindedly moved a beach bag from one place to the other. "Did I?"

"Yeah. It was pretty clear something was bothering you."

Jack gave him a grin. "Everything's okay."

Clay frowned. It didn't seem like everything was okay. Even now, Jack was acting strange.

"If there's something you'd like to talk about, you know I'm here, right?"

"Of course." Jack shrugged. "I'm good, though. Hey—there's Carrie and Emma."

Clay turned toward the shoreline and saw the women approaching.

Emma was wearing a sundress and flip-flops. Sunglasses covered her eyes, but he could see by the tilt of her mouth that she was uneasy.

Either this was going to be uncomfortable or it wasn't. It all depended on how they treated one another. Clay decided he would act like nothing had happened.

"Hey," he called out to them. "How did the meeting with the wedding planner go?"

Carrie smiled. "Wonderful. Liv has everything under control—even if she won't tell me who's making my wedding cake. She told me not to worry about it and to trust her."

"She's one of the best planners in the business," Emma said.

"I know." Carrie tossed her hand as if waving away the worry. "Right now I'm going to stop thinking about the wedding for a little while and have some fun."

They stopped near the boat, and Jack reached up to help his fiancée inside.

Clay looked up at Emma and offered her his hand.

She took it and climbed into the back of the boat.

It felt good to touch her again.

"Hello," Clay said as soon as she stood in front of him.

"Hi."

"Are we ready?" Jack asked.

"I am!" Carrie took the spot next to the driver's seat, which left the back bench to Emma and Clay.

"I'll unhook us," Clay offered as he untethered the boat from the dock.

Jack lowered the prop and then started the motor. After it warmed up for a couple seconds, he pulled away from the dock and headed toward the open water.

Clay sat next to Emma on the back bench. The wind made it difficult to talk, so he simply closed his eyes and let the wind rush past him. Sunshine warmed his face and shoulders. He took a deep breath, thankful for this respite away from all his responsibilities. It was hard to fathom that he would be back to work on Monday and this would all be a memory.

But at the moment, he was here. Next to Emma. And he would enjoy himself.

When he opened his eyes, he found Emma watching him.

She looked embarrassed at being caught and glanced away.

For over an hour, they took turns driving the boat and pulling each other on the water skis. They had all grown up on a lake, so they were experienced skiers. It was yet another thing Clay had in common with Emma.

As Jack drove the boat and Emma skied, it was Clay's turn to admire Emma. She had an athletic form and was graceful, on and off the skis.

After they finished skiing, they found an island and tethered the boat while they ate their lunch.

The cooler was brimming with good food. The cook had filled it with sandwiches, potato salad, fruit, cake and pasta salad. There were chips, cookies and cool beverages, too.

When they were done eating, Clay kicked up his heels and leaned back. "I could get used to this."

"Me, too." Emma still sat next to him. Her hair was wet from the water and her skin was glistening.

"I think Jack and I are going to explore the island a little bit," Carrie said as she started to climb out of the boat. "Do you two mind?"

Clay shook his head as Emma said no.

Soon, Jack and Carrie had disappeared into the woods on the island, leaving Emma and Clay alone in the boat. It rose and fell on the gentle waves of the lake while a soft wind ruffled the hem of Emma's sundress.

This was an opportunity Clay hadn't expected, but he would jump on it.

"I'm sorry about last night, Emma."

She glanced out at the lake. "You don't need to apologize."

"I want to." He lowered his feet and turned so he was looking at her.

They were sitting close to each other, but he refrained from touching her again.

He wanted to—but he wouldn't.

"We only just met. And given our pasts, I know I pushed you too hard."

"You didn't push me, Clay." There was longing in her voice, and she looked like she wanted to reach out to him, too, but refrained. "I just need more time."

"I understand."

She looked like she doubted him, but he understood.

"Can we talk again after the wedding?" she asked. "When things are back to normal?"

"Of course." There were only a few days left. He could wait a few days.

"There's just a lot of things I want to talk about," she continued.

"And we can't talk about them now?"

Emma shook her head. "It's too complicated now."

Her comment confused him, but he didn't ask her to elaborate. He didn't want to frustrate her or rush her.

She surprised him when she reached out and took his hand.

Her touch was soft and tentative, so he grasped her hand to let her know that she didn't need to doubt him.

"I care about you," she said gently, "and I don't want to hurt you."

"You could never hurt me, Emma." But even as he said the words, he knew they weren't true. If he had learned anything in life it was that humans, even with the best of intentions, had a devastating capability of hurting each other. Even if she never intended to, there was a very real possibility that she could hurt him.

"I would never do it on purpose," she said. "Please know that."

Clay frowned, not sure what she was talking about, but he nodded. "I do."

"Good." She slowly let go of his hand.

He wanted to reach for her again, but he didn't. His desire to kiss her was still strong—but things were complicated enough already. The last thing they needed was for him to do something foolish, like kiss her.

Or tell her that he was afraid he was falling in love with her.

Chapter Eleven

Emma couldn't remember the last time she had felt this relaxed or happy. Spending the afternoon on the boat was the best way to finish her vacation before the busyness of the wedding weekend got into full swing. And it had given her and Clay time to clear the air after last night's almost-kiss. Though there was still tension, at least they had gotten over the initial awkwardness and had openly talked about what had happened.

Carrie and Jack were gone for another twenty minutes before they reemerged from the woods and decided to head back to the resort.

"I don't want this to end," Emma said to Clay as they neared the resort, the wind pushing and tugging her hair.

"We still have a few more days before reality rushes back." He paused when his cell phone dinged.

Emma watched him read the message and saw his face go from relaxed to anxious.

"Everything okay?" she asked.

"Willow woke up from her nap with a fever."

"A fever?" Emma sat up straighter as the boat slowed.

"It's 102.4," Clay said. "She's been crying for the past twenty minutes."

"Can you hurry?" Emma asked Jack.

"I'll do my best without ramming the boat into the dock." Jack maneuvered it around buoys and other watercraft until they neared the dock.

Clay began to gather their things around him, but Carrie said, "Leave everything. We'll clean out the boat. You need to get to Willow."

"Thanks." He stood and grabbed the dock post.

Emma's pulse had jumped at the news that Willow was sick. She wanted to join Clay to make sure everything was okay, but it wasn't her place. Willow wasn't her baby, and Clay was a capable doctor. He would know what signs to look for to determine what was wrong. He didn't need her.

Yet she wanted to go.

Clay climbed out of the boat and then turned to Emma, offering her his hand.

"You want me to come?" she asked.

"Will you?"

Emma didn't hesitate. She took the hand he offered and climbed out of the boat with him.

"We'll take your things to your rooms!" Carrie called out to them. "Let us know how she's doing and if you need anything."

Clay and Emma thanked them and walked quickly toward shore.

"Has she been exposed to any viruses that you know of?" Emma asked.

"Nothing I'm aware of—but she has been prone to ear infections. I wish I'd brought my otoscope to look in her ears."

"I have one."

He glanced at her, clearly surprised. "You carry medical supplies around with you?"

"Yes." She smiled, teasing. "Don't you?"

"No."

"I have a first aid kit I keep in my car, and I added a few things to it, like an otoscope, stethoscope and digital thermometer. I'm happy to grab it."

"That would be great. Thanks, Emma."

By the time they were inside, the sound of Willow's cries could be heard out in the hallway. Emma's heart broke for the baby. She hated that Willow was in pain but couldn't tell them where it hurt.

As soon as they entered the childcare room, Willow took one look at Clay and began to cry harder. Her eyes were red and glossy, her nose was running and her cheeks were bright red. She reached for Clay, and he took her into his arms, holding her close as he spoke soothing words to her.

"Daddy's here," he said, rocking her back and forth.

Willow still cried, but her tears started to subside as she laid her cheek against his shoulder.

Emma's heart warmed at the sight of such a tall, muscular man comforting such a tiny, helpless baby.

"It's okay, Willow," Clay said. "Daddy will make it all better."

"Thank you," Emma said to the lady who had been caring for Willow.

"I didn't want to give her any Tylenol or ibuprofen without your permission," the lady said as she handed Emma the diaper bag. "And I tried getting her to eat something, but she's been crying like this since she woke up. I'm sorry I couldn't be more helpful."

"It's okay," Emma assured her. "We'll see what's causing her fever and try to get her to eat something."

"Thank you," Clay said to the caregiver as he turned to leave the room.

Emma followed and put her hand on Willow's forehead to feel for the fever.

Willow's skin was burning.

"Poor baby," Emma said. "She looks miserable."

"I hate when she feels this way. Even though it's my job to make people better, when it comes to my own daughter, I feel so helpless."

Willow's tears had subsided to a soft whimper. She pressed her fist to her mouth and took shuddering breaths.

"Has she started to teethe?" Emma asked.

"Not that I've noticed."

Emma's mind went through all the usual culprits as they climbed the stairs and went to Clay's room.

The air-conditioning in the building made Emma's skin ripple with goose bumps, and she wished she had brought a cardigan to throw over the sundress. But at the moment, all she wanted was to make Willow feel better.

When Willow was finally calm, she noticed Emma and reached for her.

Emma took Willow out of Clay's arms and went to the couch to sit with her.

"You can use whatever you find in my kit," Emma said, more concerned about comforting Willow than diagnosing her at the moment.

Clay washed his hands and then went to Emma's bag and found the otoscope, the stethoscope and the thermometer. He came to the living area and squatted in front of Emma and Willow.

"She's not going to like this part," Clay said. "She never does."

Emma was holding Willow on her lap, so Clay had to get close to them as he put the otoscope into Willow's ear.

And he was right. Willow tried to turn away, fussing again, but Emma held her in place, whispering soothing words.

Clay looked into one ear and then the other.

"Both ears look clear."

He tried to look at her throat, but it was almost impossible to get Willow to cooperate.

"From what I could see, her throat looks good, too."

"I'm happy to hear that," Emma said, very aware of Clay's nearness. He smelled like sun and waves, with a hint of cologne.

"Do you want to look?" he asked her.

"I don't think I'll see anything you didn't." Emma completely trusted Clay's abilities but appreciated his offer.

Next, he took Willow's temperature on the forehead. "It's 103.1. We should get her some Tylenol to try to bring it down. I have some in her diaper bag."

Willow seemed to like the taste of the Tylenol and drank it without any trouble.

After Clay put the dropper back into the bottle, he put the stethoscope up to his ears and listened to Willow's heart and lungs for several moments.

Emma watched him, admiring the slope of his cheeks and the intelligence in his brow. He didn't notice her as he concentrated on listening. But she didn't mind. It gave her a moment to study him.

When he finished, he pulled the stethoscope out of his ears and wrapped it around the back of his neck. He frowned as he looked at Willow. "It all sounds good to me."

"Do you think maybe she's teething?"

Clay put his finger in Willow's mouth and pressed against her gums. "They feel swollen and they're a little red. I suppose she could be—though that fever is higher than I'd like for teething."

"Maybe she just has a virus," Emma suggested. "If nothing else is obvious, we'll just need to keep alternating Tylenol and ibuprofen and make sure she's hydrated."

"That's what I was thinking, too." Clay touched Willow's cheek. "That's probably all we can do for her right now, unless she shows other signs or symptoms."

Willow looked like she was going to fall asleep again in Emma's arms. She had nestled into Emma's side and didn't seem like she wanted to go anywhere else.

"I'll make her a fresh bottle and see if she'll drink something for us." Clay stood and went to the kitchenette.

"Do you have a rocking chair in your bedroom?" Emma asked him.

"I do. I'll get it when I'm done with the bottle."

Emma hummed gently to Willow as they waited, and the baby's eyes started to droop closed.

When Clay finished the bottle, he brought it to Emma. She was able to coax Willow into drinking some of it while Clay got the rocking chair out of the bedroom.

"Do you want me to take her?" Clay asked Emma.

She shook her head and moved from the couch to the rocking chair. "If you don't mind, I'll keep her."

"I don't mind." He sat on the couch nearby. "It's kind of nice to have the help."

Emma smiled at Clay and gently rocked Willow. She used her free hand to trace the baby's cheeks and forehead, wishing she could take away her pain.

Neither Clay nor Emma spoke for a while. She was happy Willow was eating and that she seemed to be feeling a little better.

Eventually, Willow fell asleep and the Tylenol kicked in, bringing her temperature down to 99.9 degrees.

"If there's something else you need to do," Clay said, "I can take her."

"Do you mind if I stay for a bit longer?" Emma asked.

Clay studied Emma for a moment and then shook his head. "You can stay as long as you'd like, Emma."

She snuggled Willow a little closer. There was plenty to do for the wedding, and if she went back to her room now, Carrie would put her to work. But this was exactly where she wanted to be.

Clay's phone dinged, and he went to the kitchenette to check who had texted him.

"It's Jack. He's wondering how Willow is feeling and wants to know if we're going to join them for supper in the dining room. I'll let him know I can't since I'll need to stay with Willow. Would you like me to tell them what you plan to do?"

Emma didn't want to leave Willow—or Clay.

"Would you mind if I stayed and helped you with her?"

"I would love if you stayed." He smiled and then typed something into his phone. When he was done, he set his phone down and came back to the living area. "If you get hungry, let me know, and we can order room service for supper."

"I'm good for now."

And she was—in almost every way possible. There was just one thing hanging over her head, niggling at her conscience, but she couldn't do anything about it for now, so she chose to push it out of her mind and pretend everything was perfect in her little world.

Because at the moment, it was.

The sun was sending out its last rays of light as Clay finished getting dressed after taking a shower. Earlier, after Willow's temperature had dropped, Emma had gone back to her room to shower and change out of her swimsuit. She'd come back thirty minutes later with the place cards that she needed to finish for the wedding, and she had told Clay she could keep an eye on Willow while he showered.

He had been eager to get cleaned up after being in the lake and had thrown on a pair of lounge pants and a T-shirt. They had ordered supper thirty minutes before he'd showered, and he could smell the aroma of spaghetti and marinara sauce seeping into the bedroom.

Warmth filled Clay's chest, knowing that Emma was in his living room and that she would eat supper with him. After tonight, the rest of the wedding party would be at the lodge and they would have the rehearsal dinner tomorrow night, then the wedding on Saturday. And then it would be time to pack up and leave on Sunday.

Just a few more days—and this was the last one when they might be alone together.

Despite his resolve to put distance between them—and to try to forget about his growing feelings—he couldn't stop thinking about how much he wanted to keep Emma in his life. He decided it was ridiculous to push away the one thing he wanted most of all.

He ran a towel over his hair to dry it a little better and then combed it before turning off the bathroom light and leaving his bedroom.

Emma was at the table near the kitchenette, working diligently on the place cards. Willow was in her pack and play, sleeping peacefully for the moment. They had given her ibuprofen right after ordering supper, and it seemed to be working.

Emma glanced up from her work and let her gaze trail over Clay's appearance.

They were both in comfy clothes, and the intimacy of the moment didn't escape his notice.

When Emma's gaze landed on Clay's face, he smiled at her and she returned it. Her brown eyes sparkled with awareness, and he felt drawn to her, though he forced himself to stay where he was.

He wanted nothing more than to be next to her, to pull her into his arms and find out what it would be like to kiss her after all.

Instead, he glanced at the food, sitting on a tray on the counter.

"Ready to eat?"

"Sure." She put the place cards to the side and made space on the table.

Clay brought the tray to her. The table was just big enough for the two of them.

"Are you almost done with the place cards?"

"Almost. It shouldn't take me much longer to finish them."

"Good."

"Why? Did you have something else in mind?"

"I thought maybe we could watch a movie tonight. It would be a nice way to wind down after a busy day."

"I'd like that."

Clay took a seat at the table, said a prayer and then they ate their supper. Their conversation swung from one topic to the other. The more he came to know Emma, the more he liked her.

"Why did you decide to become a doctor?" she asked him as she finished her spaghetti.

"When I was younger, my sister was really sick with viral meningitis and spent almost a week in the hospital." He wiped his mouth and put his napkin on the table. "I was afraid she was going to die—and I think my parents were, too, though they stayed strong for all of us during her illness. The only thing that brought me comfort were the doctors and nurses who were taking care of her. They were compassionate yet confident, and I knew if anyone could make my sister get better, it was them."

Emma smiled as she listened to him talk.

"Of course," Clay continued, "now that I'm older, I know our lives lie in God's hands, but He has given us brains and knowledge and advancements that make healing a whole lot easier."

"And that's why you decided to become a doctor? Because of your sister's illness?"

Clay nodded. "I knew, from the age of about eight, that I wanted to make other children feel safe and protected."

"That's a very noble calling."

"I don't pretend to be noble—but I try to do my job well."

Emma's gaze was soft as she regarded him.

He leaned forward. "And what about you? Why did you decide to go into medicine?"

"We had a neighbor who was a doctor," she said. "He was an older gentleman who was already retired by the time I was old enough to know what he had done for a living. He was like a grandfather to Carrie and me, and we'd often invite him over for supper and holiday meals." Emma's eyes lit up as she spoke. "I loved hearing him tell stories about his life. He made house calls in the early years and had a clinic right in his home. I thought he was one of the smartest men I'd ever met." She laughed as she shook her head. "And I wanted to have neat stories to tell little kids one day, too."

Clay chuckled. "Isn't it amazing how one life can impact so many others?"

"I think everyone impacts more lives than they realize." Emma pushed her plate back and laid a hand on her stomach. "I'm stuffed. I don't think I'll need to eat again for a week."

"It was good." Clay put their plates and silverware back on the tray and then set it out in the hallway for housekeeping to pick up.

Emma pulled out the place cards and quickly finished them while Clay checked on Willow and then turned on the television to see what movies might be playing.

"Do you like older movies or newer ones?" he asked.

"I'm not picky—but something light and funny, please. I've had enough drama in my life to last me for years."

Clay smiled to himself, knowing exactly what she meant.

He found a nineties rom-com with Julia Roberts that was just starting. "Are you a fan of *My Best Friend's Wedding*?"

"Love it."

A few minutes later, she sighed and stood, stretching her back. "Finished."

"Ready to relax?"

"Sounds perfect."

Emma stopped at the pack and play and looked down at Willow for a few seconds. Her face looked so gentle as she studied the baby.

Clay couldn't focus on the movie. All he could think about was Emma.

"She's so beautiful," Emma said quietly. "I could look at her all night. I hope she feels better tomorrow."

"So do I. My parents will be here tomorrow, and they'll want to spend time with her."

Emma finally left Willow's crib and hesitated for a second before taking the spot next to him on the couch.

He didn't blame her, not after last night.

She sat next to him, though there were about six inches of space between them.

Clay turned up the volume a couple of notches, and they watched the movie for a few minutes in silence.

But Clay wasn't paying attention to the TV. How could he when Emma was sitting so close to him? Was she as aware of him as he was of her?

He shifted on the couch, and then she shifted.

She placed her hand on the spot between them, and he saw it out of the corner of his eye. It took all his willpower not to reach out and touch her—to see if she'd allow him to hold her hand again.

Finally, it became too much—and he gave in.

Slowly, he laid his hand next to hers, allowing his pinky finger to cross hers.

Emma looked at him, and he met her gaze. He knew what was in his mind and heart, and he longed for her to know it, too. It didn't make sense—and he knew he was risking everything, but he had to let her know. He was deluding himself if he thought he could push this away any longer.

"I can't be near you and not want to touch you, Emma."

The look in her eyes was filled with the same longing he felt. He knew why he was holding back, but he didn't know what was keeping her from allowing this thing between them to grow.

He moved closer to her, entwining her fingers with his.

"If you want me to stop, I will," he said.

She swallowed, and her chest rose and fell. "I don't want you to stop," she whispered. "That's what scares me the most."

Clay put his free hand on her cheek. He was

so close to her again—close enough that if he simply leaned forward, he would finally know what it felt like to kiss Emma's lips.

But he hesitated, waiting for her to indicate what she wanted.

"Nothing has changed, Clay," she said, looking at his lips and then meeting his gaze, driving him to distraction. "The reasons I pulled away last night are still the same reasons I should pull away now."

"What are those reasons, Em?" He leaned his forehead against hers, forcing himself not to kiss her.

"It's too soon."

"Why?"

She didn't respond right away, and he closed his eyes.

"We're afraid," she whispered.

"Because we have a lot to risk—but doesn't that also mean we have a lot to gain?"

Emma put her hands on Clay's chest, and he put his hands over hers. His heart was beating so fast, he was certain she could feel it.

"I want to kiss you, Emma," he whispered.

"I want to kiss you, too." But her hands remained on his chest, with just enough pressure to know that she wasn't ready for him to continue. And he loved and respected her too much to pressure her when she wasn't ready.

Clay took several deep breaths and then slowly pulled back from her.

She blinked as her eyes focused on him, and what he saw in their depths was both longing and turmoil. Something was keeping her from moving forward, though what it was he could only guess.

"Are you reluctant because of Tyler?" he asked, not angry or upset, though he was disappointed.

Slowly, Emma nodded. She looked torn—as if she wanted to tell him something but didn't know how to say it.

"Whatever it is, you can tell me, Emma."

She took a couple of calming breaths and then lowered her hands away from his chest. "You're like a magnet," she said. "I can't allow myself to get too close to you, or all of a sudden, I'm unable to resist your pull."

He smiled. "I can say the same about you."

"I thought we were going to wait until after the wedding to discuss this."

Clay groaned and took her hand into his again. He brought it up to his lips and pressed a kiss to the backside. "I'm an impatient man, Emma. At least where you're concerned."

"Can we just hold hands?" she asked. "And try not to be impatient?"

He chuckled. "I can try—but I don't know if I can make any promises."

Emma leaned her head on his shoulder and lowered their clasped hands.

Clay laid his cheek against the top of her head, wanting to always honor Emma and her wishes.

He cared deeply for her—was willing to admit he was falling in love with her—and he knew that he would wait for her to be ready, no matter how long it might take.

Chapter Twelve

Emma slowly woke up on Friday morning and laid in bed for several minutes with a smile on her face. She marveled at the sense of happiness that she hadn't experienced in over a year, and it was all due to Clay and Willow.

"My wedding is tomorrow," Carrie said in a sleepy voice next to Emma. "I can't believe we're finally here."

Emma rolled onto her side and smiled at her sister. It had been years since they had shared a bedroom. "Are you nervous?"

Carrie grinned. "Not in the slightest."

"Good. You should try to enjoy every moment."

"I am." Carrie turned and grabbed her phone to look at the time. She quickly sat up. "Mom and Dad texted twenty minutes ago and said they were thirty minutes away from the lodge. They'll be here for breakfast."

Emma sat up, excited to see her parents. It had been months since they'd all been together.

And they would meet Clay and Willow for the first time.

"I'll let them know they can meet us in the lobby," Carrie said. "How long before you're ready?"

"Twenty or thirty minutes."

Carrie's phone dinged, and she read the text. "Mom said they'll check into their room and meet us downstairs in forty-five minutes."

"Perfect." Emma jumped out of bed and quickly showered so Carrie could get into the bathroom next.

When Emma was ready, she called out to Carrie, "I'm going to see if Willow is feeling better. I'll meet you downstairs."

"Okay. Invite Clay to join us for breakfast if Willow's up to it."

"I will."

Emma walked down the hallway to Clay's door. She had left his room right after the movie had ended the night before. At the time, Willow had seemed to be doing better. Hopefully she was back to herself this morning.

She knocked on the door and waited for a

couple seconds until it opened. Clay stood on the other side, dressed and ready for the day, with Willow on his hip.

"Good morning," Emma said.

Willow saw Emma and reached for her.

"Good morning." Clay handed the baby to her, a smile on his face. "You look nice."

Her cheeks warmed at his praise. "Thank you." She looked over Willow to see if there were any other signs of illness or infection and tried to ignore the emotions that churned up from Clay's compliment. She didn't want to encourage him more than she already had, so she didn't comment on how good he looked— or how her heart fluttered to see him again. In forty-eight hours, she could tell him the truth about Tyler and Willow, but until then, she needed to keep her thoughts and feelings to herself. "How's our patient this morning?"

"She seems to be feeling fine. I haven't given her any Tylenol or ibuprofen since you left last night, and her fever hasn't come back. I don't know what was wrong with her, but it seems to be gone."

Emma kissed Willow's cheek, thankful she was feeling better. "My parents are here. I was just on my way down to the lobby to meet up with them for breakfast." She paused, feeling nervous, though she wasn't sure why. "Would you like to join us and meet them?"

"I'd love to meet your parents."

Warmth filled Emma's chest. She was eager for them to meet Clay, too, though so much depended on how he would react to her news on Sunday. She wanted her parents to like him—and for him to like them as well.

"Good." Emma couldn't hide her smile.

"We're ready to go now," he said. "I'll grab the diaper bag."

He stepped back into their room while Emma spoke to Willow in the hallway. When Clay joined them, he closed the suite door and put his hand on the small of Emma's back as they walked toward the stairs.

It was the slightest pressure, but it made Emma feel desired, protected and noticed. Heat climbed up her neck and into her cheeks.

If the presence of his hand at the small of her back could make her feel such a powerful sensation, she couldn't imagine being in his arms.

They walked down the stairs, and Emma saw her parents sitting on chairs near the massive rock fireplace. Her mom was looking at her phone, and her dad was flipping through a magazine.

Belatedly, Emma realized she was still holding Willow, approaching her parents with a handsome man they had never met. They probably would be more than curious—surprised and maybe even concerned.

"Do you want to take Willow?" Emma asked quietly.

"Sure." Clay took his daughter, but the baby cried and reached for Emma again.

The noise brought Emma's parents' heads up.

Her mom grinned and stood while her dad put the magazine down.

Willow continued to reach for Emma while she cried, so Emma had no choice but to take the baby back, no matter how curious her parents might be.

"Emma!" her mom said as she extended her arms, tossing a look in Clay's direction. She hugged both Emma and Willow. "And who is this little sweetie?"

"This is Willow," Emma said, trying not to feel emotional, knowing this was Tyler's baby and not being able to tell her mom. She had told her mom almost everything since she was a kid. To keep this from her was more difficult than Emma had anticipated.

"Hey, kiddo," her dad said as he, too, gave Emma and Willow a hug.

Willow stared at Emma's parents and leaned

her cheek into Emma's shoulder, looking uncertain.

"Hi, Dad." Emma loved seeing her parents again. Her dad was tall and slim, while her mom was short and petite. She looked like an older version of Emma and Carrie, though she was shorter than her daughters. Because of her parents' height difference, they had always looked like a mismatched couple—though they couldn't have been more compatible. "Mom and Dad, this is Clay Foster—Jack's cousin and best man. And this is his daughter, Willow, who has taken a liking to me this week."

"Hi, Clay," her dad said as he put out his hand. "It's nice to meet you."

"And you, too, Mr. Holt."

"Call me Brian," her dad said with a welcoming smile.

"And I'm Lucy," her mom said as she extended her hand to Clay.

When he shook it, she laughed and said, "How about a hug? I'm a hugger. Are you?"

Clay grinned and nodded. "I love hugs." He had to bend down to give Emma's mom a hug, but when he did, her smile was brilliant.

She winked at Emma over his shoulder.

Emma had missed her parents.

"And what about this little one?" her mom

asked after they broke their hug. "Willow, did you say?"

"Yes," Clay nodded, his pride for his daughter evident. "She's six months old."

Emma's mom reached out and stroked Willow's downy-soft hair. "She's beautiful. Will we be meeting her mom this weekend?"

Emma glanced at Clay, who continued to smile, though Emma could see the tightening around his eyes.

"Willow's mom is no longer a part of our lives," Clay said. "She won't be here."

"I'm sorry to hear that." Empathy filled her mom's gaze as she put her hand on Clay's arm. "What a difficult time it must be for you."

"It has been hard," Clay glanced at Emma, "but it's getting better."

Her parents shared a look, but neither one said anything. They only smiled.

"Mom!" Carrie called out as she reached the bottom of the stairs with Jack. She rushed across the lobby in a flurry of excitement. "You're here! It's getting so real!"

There were more hugs all around, and then Carrie directed everyone toward the stairs leading to the dining room. "I'm starving. Let's go eat."

Clay and Emma were at the back of the group, and Willow was still in Emma's arms.

"Your parents seem really nice, Emma," Clay said. "I can't remember the last time I got such a great hug."

"My mom's hugs are famous." Emma smiled, her heart warming. "Almost as famous as her cooking. Her two love languages are hugs and food."

"I think we're going to get along great." Clay grinned. "You look just like her."

Emma wanted to smile, too, but every time she got excited about the prospect of a future with Clay and Willow, a sinking feeling settled over her. She was looking forward to Carrie and Jack's wedding—but she wanted it to be over so she and Clay could finally talk.

They entered the dining room, and Clay brought a high chair over to the table. Emma set Willow into the chair and secured the straps while Clay pulled a bib out of the diaper bag and put it around Willow's neck. Emma took out rice-puff treats and set some on the table, while Clay pushed the high chair to the head of it, close enough for Willow to grab her food.

Her mom stood to the side, watching them quietly. When she caught Emma's gaze, she lifted a questioning eyebrow.

Emma shook her head, just slightly, though her mom wouldn't ask anything embarrassing while they were sitting with Clay. But she knew that look. As soon as they were in private, her mom would have a lot of questions for her.

"May I sit next to Willow?" her mom asked. "It's been so long since I've spent time with a little one her age."

"You help in the church nursery every chance you get," her dad reminded her.

"But we don't have one this little in the nursery," she countered. "The youngest is already a year old."

"I'm sure Willow would love that," Clay said, indicating a spot near the baby.

Emma's mom lifted her shoulders in excitement and sat next to Willow, talking to her as if they were old friends.

Clay smiled at Emma and touched the small of her back again as he moved around her to take his seat.

A delightful shiver ran up Emma's spine at his touch. She took the chair across from her mom, on the other side of Willow, and Clay sat next to her.

Again, that sense of happiness overwhelmed her, filling her with more peace than she'd felt for a long, long time. She had craved this kind of belonging, of being needed and desired.

And in that ordinary moment, as everyone settled around the table, looking over the menus, Emma realized that everyone she cared about most in the world was in one spot. Her mom and dad, Carrie and Jack, and Clay and Willow. Because somehow, in a very short amount of time, she had fallen for Clay Foster.

She watched him interact with her family as if he'd always been a part of them. It helped that he and Jack had known each other their whole lives and he already knew Carrie—but he warmed to Emma's mom and dad, and they seemed to really like him, too. Her mom paid more attention to Willow than she did the rest of them, and the baby took a shining to Emma's mom like she had to Emma.

Clay casually rested his arm along the back of Emma's chair, surprising her. When she looked up at him, while all the others were distracted in their own conversations, he smiled at her.

He didn't need to say a word; she seemed to know what he was thinking and feeling. He belonged there. Both him and Willow. They fit like the missing pieces of a puzzle, not only with her family but with her. That was why she had developed feelings for him so quickly. The pieces clicked together naturally, as if they had been made for each other.

Clay leaned forward to whisper in her ear.

Breathless, she leaned in to hear.

"I like you, Emma Holt," he said. "And I like your family, too."

It was the greatest compliment he could have given her. He hadn't even said anything embarrassing or intimate, but her cheeks filled with heat nonetheless. And when she glanced up, she saw her mom watching them.

She didn't look concerned or worried, just curious—and pleased.

But what would she think when she learned about Willow? Would she advise Emma to back away from Clay and let him lead his own life?

A sinking feeling in the pit of her stomach told Emma that was *exactly* what her mother would say.

By Friday evening, it felt like the entire resort had been overtaken by the wedding party and guests. Clay ran into friends and family members every time he left his suite. Some of them he hadn't seen in years, though everyone seemed to know about his divorce. Thankfully, Willow was feeling much better and she was happy to be passed around as people arrived. Clay's aunts and uncles were especially eager to meet her.

The only thing that put a damper on the day was that he hadn't seen Emma since breakfast. She was busy helping her sister and mom with last-minute responsibilities, so he had resigned himself to the fact that he probably wouldn't see her much until the wedding was over.

At lunchtime, so many people had joined them that they had taken up five tables in the dining room. Emma had come in late, and by the time she had arrived, all the spots at Clay's table had been taken. She'd caught his eye and they'd shared a smile, but that had been about all.

Before he'd been done eating, all the bridesmaids had left with Carrie, so Clay hadn't gotten a chance to speak to Emma then, either. He'd planned to work on the wedding cake after lunch and had hoped that she could help him, but he knew she was busy. And the truth was he could decorate the cake on his own.

He dropped Willow off with childcare and then spent most of the afternoon in the kitchen, putting the cake together. It was three tiers high, covered in white frosting with a green band of fondant around the bottom of each tier that Emma had assured him would match her bridesmaid dress.

Clay's specialty had been fondant flowers, and so he made several to put on the cake. It was detailed, concentrated work, but he enjoyed it. He loved working with his hands and having something to keep him busy while allowing himself to think about Emma.

He couldn't wait to see her in her dress tomorrow—to walk with her down the aisle, sit with her at the head table and hold her in his arms during the wedding dance. They would have time together—something he was coming to treasure more than anything, especially now that there were so many other people at the resort.

It took him several hours to decorate the cake, and when he was finished, he realized he didn't have much time left to get ready for the wedding rehearsal. They were supposed to arrive at the lakeside to rehearse at five, with a meal following.

Clay had scheduled childcare for most of the day, so he left the kitchen and went up to his room to shower and dress for the evening. He had texted the caregiver a few times that afternoon to make sure Willow was still feeling okay. He'd been reassured that Willow was doing just fine.

After Clay got out of the shower, he changed into a pair of charcoal-gray trousers and a white button-down shirt, which he rolled at the sleeves. As he was putting on his belt, his phone dinged. He was happy to see it was a text from his mom telling him that they had arrived at the resort. She wanted to know where she could find her granddaughter.

His parents knew Willow wasn't his biological child, but it didn't matter to them. As soon as Clay had decided he was going to raise Willow as his own, they had embraced her, too.

He texted his mom and told her he'd pick Willow up from childcare and meet them in the lobby in ten minutes.

As he finished getting ready, he couldn't help but feel excited that Emma was going to meet his mom and dad. They meant the world to him, and he hoped they would like her. Emma's parents had been great, and he even suspected that his parents would get along with hers.

When he was finally ready, he grabbed his cell phone and left his room—and almost bumped into Emma as she came out of hers.

Clay's breath caught, both from surprise and from seeing Emma in a black cocktail gown.

She had twisted her hair up in the back and was wearing a pair of sparkling black earrings and tall, black heels.

He'd never seen anyone so beautiful in his life.

She seemed just as surprised as him. "Hello."

They were alone in the dim hallway, standing close.

"Hello," he said quietly. "You look stunning, Emma."

Her smile completely unraveled what little composure he had, and his heart started to pound hard. How was he going to get through the next twenty-four hours without talking about the thing he wanted to talk about most in the world?

Their future.

"You look very handsome yourself," she said.

He wished they didn't have to join the others.

"I'm heading down to get Willow." He tried not to sound breathless. "My parents are here and want to spend time with her this evening."

"Your parents are here?" she asked.

He nodded. "Would you like to meet them?"

She studied him with her dark brown eyes, so many emotions flooding her gaze.

"I'd like you to meet them," he said gently. "I think they're going to love you."

"I'd like to meet them, too." She reached up to adjust his collar.

He loved feeling the gentle touch of her hand against his neck, and he couldn't help but capture her wrist, pulling her hand to his lips.

"I wish you could feel my heartbeat, Emma."

She studied him and took a deep breath.

"Whenever you're near me," he said, "I can't think of anything else. And when you're not near me, I can't think of anything else."

She lowered her gaze to look at his mouth. Without warning, she stood on tiptoe and placed a lingering kiss on his cheek.

"We'll talk on Sunday," she whispered. "I promise."

He let her go and nodded. "I'm counting down the hours."

Emma slipped her hand into his and then led him toward the stairs. Before they turned at the landing, she let him go.

Clay's parents were standing in the lobby. His mom's face lit up with joy at the sight of him.

She kissed his cheek when he reached her side. "Clay! Where is that grandbaby of mine?"

"I'm on my way to get her now."

"And who is this?" his dad asked, smiling at Emma.

She had moved a discreet distance away from Clay—but more than anything, he wanted to put his arm around her and draw her as close as he could and tell his parents how much she meant to him. Instead, he forced himself not to grin like a fool and said, "This is Emma Holt, Carrie's sister and the maid of honor."

"Of course you're Carrie's sister," his mom said as she smiled and offered her hand to Emma. "You look just like her. I'm Nan Foster, and this is my husband, Pete."

"It's nice to meet you," Emma said.

"And you, too." His mom smiled.

His dad shook Emma's hand next and said, "We're looking forward to welcoming your family into ours this weekend."

Clay wanted to do more than welcome Emma's family into theirs, but he kept his thoughts to himself. For now.

They went to the childcare room to get Willow. Just like before, she reached for Emma as soon as she could and nestled into Emma's shoulder. Emma gave her a hug and a kiss and then relinquished her to Clay's mom, who hadn't seen her in weeks.

"Grandma has so many presents for you in her suitcase," his mom said to Willow. "I brought a whole suitcase just for you."

"I wish you wouldn't buy her so many things," Clay said.

"I bought her a few outfits and a couple of toys. Nothing extravagant."

"She has more clothes than she'll ever be able to wear."

"Oh, pish-posh. It's a grandma's right and privilege to spoil her grandbabies." She kissed Willow's cheek. "Isn't that right, Willow?"

Clay shook his head. It didn't matter how often he told his parents to ease up on the presents, they never did.

"Emma and I need to get to the rehearsal," Clay told them.

"Go on." His mom hugged Willow again. "We'll meet you for supper later. For now, we'll take Willow to our room."

"Sounds good. Thanks, Mom."

"My pleasure."

His parents walked away with Willow, almost oblivious to anything else, leaving Clay and Emma alone.

"She seems like a devoted grandma," Emma said.

"She was born for the role." Clay focused his attention on Emma again. "I finished the cake this afternoon."

Her eyes lit up. "Can I see it? I was so bummed I couldn't help you today."

Clay glanced at his phone and saw they still had a few minutes before they were expected at the rehearsal, so he took her hand in his and nodded. "It's in the kitchen cooler."

She entwined their fingers as they walked toward the steps in the corner of the lobby.

The waitstaff was busy in the dining room setting the tables for supper as Clay and Emma wove through the room toward the kitchen.

When they got into the kitchen, the cook nodded at Clay but didn't bother to talk to them. He was busy prepping the evening meal.

For some reason, Clay cared more about what Emma thought of the cake than what Carrie and Jack would think. He let go of her hand to open the cooler door.

The cake was sitting where he had left it.

Clay watched Emma's reaction—and when her eyes lit up with delight, he couldn't help but grin.

"Clay! It's amazing!"

"Do you really like it?"

"I love it." She reached up and gave him a hug. "It looks exactly like the picture!"

Her hug surprised Clay, but he wrapped his arms around her.

"Carrie is going to love this." She pulled back. "Thank you."

"I'm happy I could come to the rescue."

Emma's eyes softened. "So am I."

If nothing else happened that day, Clay would have gone to bed feeling accomplished. Who would have guessed that a random suggestion from a professor would one day be exactly what made Emma pleased with him?

They left the kitchen and walked through the doors in the dining room to a patio facing the lake. The dancing would be held on the patio the following evening if the weather cooperated. Thankfully, the forecast looked perfect for the next day, though a storm was predicted for that evening.

Clay glanced toward the northwest and saw a wall of clouds gathering.

A few minutes later, they arrived at the wedding rehearsal. Almost everyone else had already gathered. Carrie and Jack's pastor was speaking to them near the arch where they would stand. Other wedding party members were milling around, laughing and talking. Emma's mom and dad were standing near the bride and groom, listening to the pastor's instructions.

"We should probably join the happy couple and make sure we know what we're supposed to be doing tomorrow," Emma said. She started to move away, but Clay reached out and touched her hand, stopping her.

She looked up at him, a question in her eyes.

"In case we get too busy to spend any time alone together before this is all over, I want you to know I've had a really good time this week, Emma. You're one of the best surprises of my life."

The look that passed over her face was so hard to read—but it disappeared quickly and she offered him a sad smile before walking away.

Chapter Thirteen

Emma was content to stand back and watch Carrie shine that evening. Just like Carrie had hoped, she and Jack were the center of attention, and rightfully so. Though Emma hated that she hadn't been able to say anything to Clay about Willow, perhaps Carrie had been smart to keep it quiet until after the wedding festivities.

As it was, Clay's beaming face and cheerful mood made the entire event even more enjoyable. Every time Emma glanced in his direction, he was smiling or laughing. He was fun to watch as he took the time to greet each person, making their faces light up with joy. He had the ability to make people feel special and seen—something Tyler had lacked. Emma's late husband had usually left a gathering exhausted from all the talking he had done about himself, but Clay was so different. He rarely spoke about himself, unless asked a question, and ended up being noticed and admired because of his humility and thoughtfulness.

And because he was easily the most handsome man there.

"Having fun?" her mom asked as she approached Emma where she was standing a little removed from the group on the patio, watching everyone mingle before the rehearsal dinner. She and Clay had been together during the rehearsal and would be seated next to each other for the meal, but at the moment, everyone was busy saying hello or meeting for the first time, and she enjoyed watching.

"I am," Emma said, accepting her mom's side hug as her arm wrapped around her waist.

"We haven't had a minute alone together today," her mom continued. "You can imagine that I have a lot of questions."

Emma knew her mom wouldn't let the situation with Clay go unnoticed.

"How about we take a little walk? The meal won't start for about fifteen minutes."

"Okay." Emma was eager to talk to her mom—but also a little nervous.

They walked along a flagstone path to a garden. A bench sat in the corner, so her mom led Emma there. She took a seat and then patted the bench.

Emma sat next to her mom and looked up at the sky. The sun was fading and sending off brilliant colors across the wide expanse. The oncoming storm had held off to the northwest, but lightning jumped in the clouds and promised quite the show. Thankfully, the meal would be inside, though there was a meet and greet hour on the patio beforehand.

"So," her mom said. "Let's not make small talk. I would be blind if I didn't notice what's going on with you and Clay."

Emma had always been open and honest with her mom and felt safe confiding in her, so she didn't even hesitate. "I think I'm in love with him."

A gentle smile tilted up her mom's lips. "In love? So soon?"

"He's wonderful—thoughtful and kind. And we get along so well and have so many things in common."

"Including heartbreak?"

Emma nodded. "I felt close to him from the start because of our shared heartbreak."

"I can tell he feels the same way about you— but has he told you?"

"He keeps trying to, but I want to wait until after the wedding to discuss our feelings."

Her mom tilted her head and frowned. "Why?"

This was the part she had dreaded telling her mother, and she found herself whispering, "Willow is Tyler's baby."

For several heartbeats, Emma's mom just stared at her. When she finally seemed to pull herself together, she said, "What? How?"

Emma told her mother how she had come to realize the truth, sparing no details.

"And Clay doesn't know who Willow's father is?"

"I don't think so. But he does know she's not his biological child."

"And he chose to raise her? Even after Sadie left?"

Emma nodded, her love for Clay growing each time she thought about it.

"That's remarkable, Emma—one of the most sacrificial things I've ever heard. No wonder you've fallen in love with him." She took one of Emma's hands. "But he needs to know, honey. As soon as possible. You should have told him the second you figured it out."

"I know, but Carrie asked me not to."

"I think you've used Carrie's wedding as an

excuse, Em. This isn't her news to share—it's yours and Clay's. And, knowing more about him, I would guess that he wouldn't have allowed the news to dampen the festivities this weekend. He might be upset, and perhaps he might lose trust in you, but he wouldn't have let it ruin Carrie and Jack's wedding."

Emma knew her mom was right—and she probably had used Carrie as an excuse to avoid the discussion, prolonging the agony. But her heart beat hard as she thought about the conversation. She loved Clay and wanted him to trust her, more than anything. Could he, knowing she had kept this information from him?

"I know you're scared," her mom said as she squeezed Emma's hand. "But he'll respect you more if you tell him the truth and explain why you waited. It might take him some time to come to terms with the news, just like it took you time, but ultimately, it's not your fault or his. Tyler and Sadie were at fault." She moved a strand of hair off Emma's forehead. "I can't think of anything better than seeing you and Clay find love in the midst of the ashes and rubble Tyler and Sadie left behind. What a beautiful work of redemption from God."

"Do you think Clay will forgive me for not saying anything before now?" Emma asked.

"I can't say for sure, but I'd be shocked if he didn't. From all that you've told me, Clay Foster sounds like an honorable man."

Emma nodded. He was certainly honorable.

"It makes me happy to see that you're starting to heal," her mom said, tears in her eyes. "There's nothing harder in this world than to see your child suffer. I know how devastating this past year has been for you. It's wonderful to see God orchestrate this beautiful connection between you—and what a blessing that Willow loves you like she does."

Tears came to Emma's eyes, too. "I didn't know if I could love Willow when I first realized who she was—but I do, more than I thought possible." She wiped at one of the tears that fell down her cheek. "I thought you were going to tell me to stay out of their lives once I told you who Willow really is."

Her mom smiled. "Why would I do that?"

"Because it's messy—and because Willow is a reminder of Tyler's infidelity."

"Do you think of Tyler's infidelity when you're with Willow? Does she remind you of him?"

"She reminds me of him sometimes, but I don't think of his infidelity when I'm with her. She's a brand-new person, who shouldn't be responsible for the mistakes of her biological parents."

"Just like you and Clay shouldn't be responsible, either." She squeezed Emma's hands again. "Life is messy and chaotic, honey, but that doesn't mean we should run from the hard things. It's often in the midst of the hard things that we find our greatest purpose in life. Who knows what God has planned for your life? Maybe you'll be the one who gets to show Willow the redemptive love of God in a very real and tangible way. I would never tell you to run away from that."

Emma hoped and prayed her mom was right. Clay owed her nothing and she had no rights to Willow—but she wanted to be a part of the girl's life, just like she wanted to be a part of Clay's life.

"I'll try to talk to Clay tonight, after the rehearsal dinner," Emma said. "And if I can't find the time, then I'll wait until after the wedding."

"I hope he'll understand why you waited," her mom said. "Because even though it was an excuse, you were trying to honor your sister's wishes."

They stood and walked back to the patio, where people were still mingling.

Emma looked for Clay and saw him talking

to an older couple. He looked up at her as if he had been watching for her to return. He gave her a quizzical look, seeming to ask if she was okay, and she forced herself to smile for him. She didn't want him to be concerned. She'd talk to him soon enough, though right now all she could think about was how nervous she felt. It probably wouldn't be hard to get him alone tonight after the meal to talk.

The sound of silverware clinking glass made the din of conversation fade as everyone looked toward the source of the sound.

Carrie and Jack stood, holding hands, in front of the sliding glass doors leading into the dining room. Carrie was wearing a white cocktail gown with white heels, and her dark hair was curled around her shoulders. Emma had never seen her look so happy. It made her happy, too.

"Thank you all for coming," Carrie said. "Jack and I are blessed to have you share this special weekend with us. Thank you especially to my sister, Emma, who came to the resort early to help, and to Clay, Jack's cousin, for his help. We want to thank our parents as well and our entire wedding party for all they've done."

There was a round of applause, and when it died down, Jack said, "And now I'd like to

thank my parents for hosting the groom's dinner and ask that everyone bow their heads with
me as we thank God for this meal we're about
to eat and for this wedding we're going to celebrate tomorrow."

As Jack prayed, Emma couldn't help but
offer her own thanksgiving. She also prayed
that God would give her the right words to communicate with Clay—and, more than anything,
that Clay would find it in his heart to forgive
her for not telling him about Willow sooner.

"Amen," Jack said as he finished his prayer.
Clay echoed, "Amen," and looked up to see
where Emma was standing. She had disappeared with her mom for several minutes but
had just come back to join the group. He didn't
know where they had gone or what had happened, but Emma's countenance had changed.
She looked unsettled and even unhappy. Clay
hoped they hadn't been fighting, but one look
at Lucy and he was pretty sure they hadn't ar-
gued. Emma's mom looked just as happy and
composed as she had before they'd left.

As everyone started to file past Clay into the
dining room, he waited for Emma to reach his
side. He smiled at several people and nodded at
his mom, who was holding Willow, to indicate

that he was aware she still had his daughter. Clay hadn't held her once since his mom had gotten ahold of her, and he suspected it would be the same for the rest of the weekend. They had even gone into his room, with his permission, and taken Willow's pack and play into their room so Willow could sleep with them. Clay would be busy getting ready for the wedding in the morning, and they wanted him to have a good night's sleep.

Finally, Emma walked up to him—but instead of smiling, she looked uneasy.

"Everything okay?" Clay asked. He had the urge to take her hand or put his arm around her to comfort her, but he refrained.

Emma nodded. "I think so."

"I noticed that you and your mom left. Did you fight?"

"No." Emma shook her head quickly. "We just had a talk." She smiled at someone who walked past her and put her hand on Emma's shoulder in greeting. When Emma looked back at Clay, she said, "Can you and I get away this evening? After dinner, maybe? I'd like to talk to you."

Clay smiled down at Emma. "I would go anywhere with you. Just say the word."

She finally smiled at him—the smile he'd

been longing to see—and it went straight to his heart. He marveled at the effect she had on him.

"Should we go eat?" he asked. "Because the sooner we get this meal over with, the sooner I get you all to myself."

She nodded, and they followed the others into the dining room, where they were directed to a private room in the back. There were close to forty people at the groom's dinner, but thankfully, there was a table reserved for the wedding party and Clay would get to sit next to Emma.

The meal was delicious and included salad, two different pasta dishes, bread and dessert. Clay ate heartily, laughing and enjoying the conversation around the table. Emma's family had quickly blended with Clay's family, and friendships were already being formed. The noise increased as friends and family started to share stories about Jack and Carrie as children and teenagers.

Emma stayed strangely quiet as she observed the activities. She wasn't sullen or upset—but she didn't join in with the banter or good-natured teasing. A sad, gentle smile softened her face, but it wasn't as carefree as he'd come to recognize and love about her.

On more than one occasion, he wanted to ask

her if she was feeling okay, but he knew she'd tell him if she wasn't.

She twisted her cloth napkin in her hands as they lay in her lap, and her face had become pale. She kept looking at the clock on the wall. He wondered what had her so uneasy because there was no other way to describe her behavior.

He was thankful they had planned to spend some time alone together after the meal so he could ask her what she was upset about.

Finally, after the dessert had been served and Jack's parents had made a speech, thanking everyone for joining them at the dinner, people began to gather up their things to leave. It was only nine o'clock, but with the wedding in the morning, many people were planning to go to bed. There would be board games in one of the aunt and uncle's rooms, and the wedding party planned to hang out near the fireplace in the lobby for a little bit to catch up. But Clay and Emma had other plans.

Emma rose to speak to her cousin from Iowa, who had arrived late, and Clay stood back and waited patiently.

Outside, the wind picked up with intensity, but there were no windows in the back room where they'd been eating, so he didn't know if it had started to rain. A peal of thunder reverberated through the dining area, suggesting that if it hadn't already, it would soon.

"Clay," Jack said as he came up behind him and put his hand on his shoulder.

Clay turned to his cousin with a grin. "Looks like everything is off to a good start."

Jack glanced in Emma's direction and then back at Clay. There was something heavy in his gaze—a look that shouldn't have been there the day before Jack's wedding.

"What's wrong?" Clay asked.

"Can I talk to you for a minute?"

"Sure." Clay glanced at Emma, who was still talking with her cousin. He hoped that whatever Jack wanted to say wouldn't take a lot of time.

Jack motioned for Clay to follow him out of the party room and into the main section of the dining room. It was empty now, and Clay could see the rain slashing against the windows in a downpour.

"What's going on?" Clay asked Jack as he followed his cousin to a corner where they would be out of the way. "Is everything all right?"

"No." Jack shook his head and let out a deep breath. "I didn't know if I should tell you—and the longer I've waited, the worse I've felt. Carrie doesn't want me to say anything until the wedding is over, but I can't live with myself right now. You're my best friend, Clay, and I don't want you to get hurt."

Dread filled Clay's gut as he stared at his cousin. "What are you talking about, Jack?"

Jack looked over Clay's shoulder, then leaned in. "It's about Willow. I learned something this week, and it's eating me alive. I knew I couldn't wait another day before I told you. I don't want anything bothering me on my wedding day."

"Willow?" Clay was confused. What would Jack know about Willow?

Jack stared at him for a couple seconds before he said, "I know who Willow's father is, Clay."

The dread felt like a millstone, causing an ache to form in Clay's gut. "How do you know who her father is? I don't even know."

Jack looked like he was going to be sick. He swallowed hard. "Willow's father was Tyler Freberg."

"Tyler Freberg?" Clay felt more confused than ever. "Should that name mean something to me? I have no idea who that is."

"Tyler was Emma's husband. Her last name used to be Freberg."

Clay stared at Jack as the information sank

in. How could it even be possible? Anger started to tighten his chest. "What are you saying?"

Jack looked over Clay's shoulder again and said quietly, "Tyler was the man Sadie was seeing when she got pregnant with Willow. He met her at the hotel where Sadie worked—at a pharmaceutical convention or something like that."

"I don't understand." Clay shook his head. "How do you know this?"

If what Jack had said was true, then that meant Emma's husband had been cheating on her with Clay's wife. The ramifications of that could shake the very foundations of the tenuous relationship Clay and Emma had built. What would Emma think when she learned the truth? Would she be devastated? Would it color her thoughts and feelings toward Clay and Willow?

Clay's anger turned to panic, realizing that Emma might turn away from him because of this.

Jack stared at Clay for a long time. "I know this is true," he said, "because Emma told me."

For a second, the world felt like it had stopped spinning and time stood still.

"What?" Clay felt sick—truly ill. "Emma knows?"

"I overheard her and Carrie talking about it the day we got here—but they didn't want you to know until after the wedding. They were afraid you'd be mad and ruin it for us. But I tried to tell them that I knew you better than that. You wouldn't ruin the wedding over something like this—right?"

"Emma knew, and she didn't want to tell me?" Betrayal sliced through Clay, opening his heart and making his wounds feel as fresh and raw as they had the day Sadie had left him. "She was afraid I'd ruin the wedding if I knew?"

He couldn't fathom Emma's heartlessness in keeping the information to herself—and then pretending nothing was wrong—just to save her sister's wedding. She had worked her way into his and Willow's hearts to try to keep them pacified, the entire time knowing that she was withholding a devastating secret.

Jack glanced over Clay's shoulder again, and his eyes opened wide at what he saw. He took a step back from Clay.

Without even looking, Clay knew Emma had come out of the party room. He closed his eyes, not wanting to turn and face her. He'd trusted her—believed that because of her own heartache, she understood the importance of trust in a relationship. Yet she had betrayed him, and though it wasn't the same betrayal as Sadie's, it was just as painful. It involved Sadie—perpetuated the lies that Sadie had started.

He felt like a fool. Just like he had when he'd learned about Sadie's unfaithfulness. Had Emma and Carrie been laughing behind his back because he hadn't known? Were they laughing now?

"Clay?" Emma asked quietly. "Can we find somewhere quiet to talk?"

It took all of Clay's willpower to turn and face Emma, and when he did, he knew he wasn't doing a good job keeping his anger and disgust hidden.

Her mouth slipped open, and her eyes revealed her surprise at his reaction. She took a step back and shook her head. "What's wrong?"

"What's wrong?" he asked, taking a step toward her, angry at her, angry at himself and angry at God for allowing him to fall in love again, only to have that love used against him. "How could you, Emma?"

Emma looked from Clay to Jack, questions in her eyes. And then it looked like it dawned on her, and she quickly turned her gaze back to Clay. "I was going to tell you—tonight." She reached out to him, but he pulled back from her.

"Don't touch me," he said. "Don't talk to me, don't come near me or Willow—"

"Clay, I can explain."

"There's no need." His voice was hard—it had to be. There was no other way he knew how to defend himself against her heartless behavior.

"I wanted to tell you," she said, tears in her eyes. "But Carrie didn't think—"

"Don't blame your sister. We spent the entire week together before she got here. You could have told me—but you didn't." He was having a hard time controlling his emotions. "Did you think it was funny?"

"Funny?" She shook her head, tears gathering in her eyes. "No. I thought it was heartbreaking and devastating—"

"How long have you known?"

"I just figured it out—the day you arrived. Believe me, Clay, I'm as shocked and horrified as you."

"Yet you thought it best if you knew and I didn't. You were afraid I would somehow ruin Carrie's wedding if I knew, right?"

Carrie appeared at the door. The wind and rain probably drowned out their heated argument from the others, but Carrie looked concerned as she approached.

Clay was just as upset at Carrie, though her decision not to tell Clay wasn't as painful as

Emma's. He had thought she cared about him, when this entire time, she had been lying to him.

"I won't ruin your wedding," Clay said to Carrie as he stood straight and lifted his chin. "I can pretend, like you two, that everything is fine. No one will suspect a thing tomorrow—and then as soon as the speeches are done, Willow and I are leaving, and none of you need to worry about seeing us again."

He moved around Emma to leave the dining room.

"Clay!" she called as she followed him.

Turning abruptly, she bumped into him and he had to catch her so she didn't fall.

When he set her upright, he removed his hands and met her stricken gaze. "Don't follow me, Emma. You're the last person I want to see right now."

And with that, Clay left the dining room and strode up the stairs to his suite.

His heart had been broken one too many times. And this time, he was going to be smarter. He wouldn't let Emma hurt him.

At least—he wouldn't let her hurt him any more than she already had.

Chapter Fourteen

EMMA stared after Clay, her heart shattering into a million little pieces. She turned on her heels and looked to Jack for an explanation.

He and Carrie stood in the back of the dining room looking dejected.

"Why did you tell him?" Emma asked, her voice just above a whisper.

Carrie's mouth slipped open, and she turned to Jack. "You told Clay? How could you? I told you I didn't want him to know."

Emma's parents had left the party room and were standing near the door—whether to block everyone else from hearing and seeing the drama unfolding or because they were stunned, she wasn't sure.

"He should have known immediately," Jack said to Carrie. "I couldn't live with myself if I didn't tell him."

"Emma was going to tell him on Sunday," Carrie said.

"That wasn't soon enough."

"Now that you've told him, he's going to hate Emma. She was the one who needed to tell him."

"This isn't my fault, Carrie. You and Emma should have taken care of this."

Emma's mom left the door and came to her side. She wrapped her arms around Emma and held her tight.

The tears flowed down Emma's face as she thought of all she had lost in an instant.

"I was going to tell him," she whispered. "Tonight—right now."

"I know, Em." Her mom pulled back, her face filled with empathy. "I'm sorry, honey."

"What's going on?" her dad asked, looking truly perplexed.

"I'll tell you later, Brian," her mom said to pacify him.

Carrie left Jack and walked over to Emma, joining their little family circle. "I'm sorry, too, Em. I didn't know Jack was going to tell Clay."

Jack stood in the corner where he and Clay had been standing, but he, too, walked over to Emma. He looked miserable—and though Emma was upset that he had told Clay before she could, she really didn't blame him. He loved Clay and was concerned for his cousin.

"You're right, Jack," Emma said, wiping her tears. "We shouldn't have kept it from Clay, but it was my news to share, and now he'll never forgive me."

"I think he will. If you give him time."

Emma shook her head. "Our wounds are deep, and the betrayal isn't easily forgotten. I added to that betrayal by not telling him right away." She knew she needed to talk to Clay, to try to make him understand. He would probably never trust her again, but at least she could try to prevent more trauma on top of all the rest.

"I'm sorry, Emma," Jack said. "I just couldn't get married tomorrow with Clay by my side, knowing this was hanging over my head."

Carrie's face filled with anger again, but before she could open her mouth to tell Jack what she thought of his actions, Emma laid her hand on Carrie's arm.

"Don't be angry at him, Care. Jack is a good man with a good heart, and he thought he was doing the right thing. Don't let this ruin your wedding day. I'm going to talk to Clay, if he'll let me, and hopefully I can fix this somehow."

She didn't have high hopes—but she had to try.

It took a couple seconds, but Carrie finally nodded.

Emma left her family in the dining room and slowly walked up the stairs. Her feet felt heavier than usual, and dread filled her with each step. Would Clay even be in his room? Would he open the door to her? She couldn't go to sleep without telling him she was sorry. But would he even listen?

She made it to the lobby level and rounded the banister to start climbing the second set of stairs. Her heart pounded so hard, it was all she could hear as she trudged along. She prayed with all her might that God would give her the right words to say to Clay. She loved him and didn't want to hurt him more than she already had. She had no hope that he would ever feel for her the way he had before—but at least she might make him understand. And she hoped he wouldn't hate her.

When she arrived in the hallway, it was dim as usual, but the sound of the raging storm outside made it feel ominous. She wanted to duck into her own room and hide away, pretending none of this had happened, but she owed it to Clay to talk to him.

Just thinking about the anger on his face when he had looked at her made her pause.

Seeing the love in his eyes fade to revulsion brought her to tears again. But she needed to hold it together for a few more minutes. When she was done speaking to him, she would have hours to cry herself to sleep.

All she could think about right now was taking away his pain.

She stood for a few seconds outside his door, inhaling a couple deep breaths, trying to get up the nerve to knock. Her greatest fear was that he would answer the door and then slam it in her face. But her second-greatest fear was that he wouldn't even open it.

Emma forced herself to lift her hand and knock.

She took a step back and waited, her breathing shallow.

Her body shook from head to toe, and even as she tried to smooth back her hair, her hands trembled so violently it was impossible.

A movement within the room made Emma pause, and then the door opened and Clay stood before her. His face was still filled with anger—but there was a sadness there, too, and it broke Emma's heart all over again.

"I told you I didn't want to see you, Emma." His voice was quieter—weaker—as if he was drained of all the fight that had been in him.

She swallowed the nerves and nodded, wiping away a stray tear with her trembling hand.

"I know I don't deserve your time," she said, "but I'm asking if you'll allow me just a few minutes to try to explain."

He studied her, his chest rising and falling. "I don't think there's anything you could say to make me understand."

Emma nodded and looked down at her hands. "I don't expect you to forgive me, Clay, but I want you to know a few things." She lifted her gaze again, feeling a little stronger. "I didn't know that Tyler had fathered a baby until the day I met you and Willow." She pressed her eyes closed for a second, reliving the pain of that moment. "And when it all came together, I was devastated. It's why I ran away from you at the beach and then why I left you at the dance. I was trying to come to terms with the fact that I hadn't been able to have a baby—only to realize that my unfaithful husband had fathered a child with someone else."

Pain sliced through Clay's face as he continued to watch her.

"When I realized who Willow was, I called Carrie to tell her. Please believe me, I wanted you to know—but Carrie didn't want the focus of her wedding to be on us. I agreed to wait to tell you, which I deeply regret. And I admit I used the wedding as an excuse not to deal with the truth, but I didn't realize it until tonight, when I was talking to my mom."

His face remained unreadable.

"I was going to tell you, Clay—it was the reason I asked to speak to you tonight. I didn't know that Jack had planned to tell you. It wasn't his place, but I can't fault him for doing my job when I failed to do it myself."

She took a deep breath, watching him, hoping to see some sort of understanding in his gaze.

"I'm sorry," she said as tears came to her eyes again. "The last thing I would ever want is to hurt you." She weighed the wisdom of her next words for only a second and decided to speak them without reservation. "I love you," she whispered.

He winced but didn't respond.

"And I love Willow," she continued. "I don't understand why all of this happened, but it did, and now we have to live with the consequences. But we don't have to keep perpetuating the pain. I hope you can learn to forgive me—even if you might never be able to trust me."

The tears were streaming down her cheeks now, and she impatiently wiped them away.

Clay shook his head and looked down at the ground, breaking eye contact with her.

"I've been hurt so many times, Emma, that I'm numb. I've forgiven, learned to trust again, and then been blindsided by betrayal." He looked up at her, his pain and heartache palpable. "I will forgive you—and I'll even try to understand why you kept the truth from me—but I don't think I can allow myself to get blindsided again. I can't be numb where Willow is concerned, so the only way I know how to protect myself is if I don't let anyone in."

They stood for a few seconds on either side of the threshold, but neither one spoke or made a move.

Finally, Clay took a step back into his room. "Good night, Emma."

She nodded as more tears fell. "Good night, Clay."

He closed his door and she turned and walked blindly toward her own room.

The tears fell so quickly, she didn't even bother to wipe them away.

She'd lost Clay and Willow, just as she had feared she would. Maybe Clay would have trusted her if she had told him first, but now she would never know.

Would she never experience joy and happiness again?

* * *

Clay adjusted his tie as he looked in the mirror one last time before leaving his room the next morning. He hadn't slept well the night before, mulling over the previous week and everything he and Emma had gone through. He tried to examine each memory to see if he could pinpoint the moments of truth and betrayal—but he struggled to see things clearly. His anger and pain concerning Emma were intermingled with his heartbreak from Sadie. It was almost impossible to separate the two and look at his relationship with Emma objectively.

With a sigh, Clay grabbed his cell phone and left his room, hoping and praying he wouldn't run into Emma in the hallway. Though he had showered and shaved and tried everything he could to be presentable for the wedding, he still looked miserable. He would have to fake happiness today for Jack and Carrie's sake and do everything in his power to make this a joyful occasion. No doubt the couple had been up late fighting over what had happened. Clay tried to understand, for Carrie's benefit, but he couldn't quite accept her reasoning. This was his daughter they were talking about—and Emma's late husband. The second Emma had started to suspect the truth, Clay should have been told. To know that she had kept it from him, while he'd shared the intimate and painful pieces of his past, hurt the most.

Thankfully, the hallway was quiet as Clay walked toward Jack's room. He had the nicest suite in the lodge—on the corner, with magnificent views of the lake.

Clay knocked and then let himself in because Jack was expecting him.

"I'm in here," Jack called to Clay from the bedroom, "trying to get this tie straight."

Clay crossed the living area and glanced at the clock. They had about twenty minutes to get to the lake for the ceremony. Everyone in the wedding party had dined separately for breakfast, since Carrie didn't want Jack to see her before the ceremony. Clay had stayed in his room, not wanting to see anyone until it was absolutely necessary. Thankfully, his mom and dad had Willow and he hadn't needed to worry about feeding her and getting her ready for the wedding.

It had just been Clay and his thoughts all morning.

He took a deep breath as he walked through the door and into the bedroom. "Need some help?"

Jack stood in front of the tall mirror. He looked a little harried as he untied his tie and shook his head. "I've wrestled with this thing for fifteen minutes."

"Let me."

Turning, Jack looked at Clay with a wary expression. "Sorry about last night."

"Yeah. I am, too." Clay adjusted the ends of the tie to lie on Jack's chest before he started to tie them.

"Carrie and I got into a big fight—which I should have expected, but it's not what you'd want to do the night before your wedding."

Clay nodded but didn't respond.

"Did Emma talk to you?"

Again, Clay nodded.

Jack looked hopeful. "Did you work things out?"

"She explained her side of the story, if that's what you mean."

Neither one spoke for a couple of seconds as Clay finished tying Jack's tie. When he was done, he stepped back and let Jack look in the mirror.

"Wow. You did that fast."

"I wear a lot of ties."

Jack lifted his black suit coat off the back of a

nearby chair and pulled it on over his arms and shoulders. He stared at himself in the mirror for a few seconds and then turned back to Clay.

"I've been thinking a lot about what I said last night and how it came across." Jack stared at Clay, his face serious. "I should have handled it differently and thought more about what I was saying."

"It was true, so what does it matter? I don't really want to talk about it, Jack."

"It was true—but I misrepresented some things. I was upset with Carrie for how she wanted to handle the situation, and I lumped Emma into the blame because I didn't want you to think less of Carrie."

Clay frowned. "What are you talking about?"

"When I told you how things had happened, I made it sound like Emma had been in on the deception. The truth is that from the start, Emma was the one who wanted to tell you. Even before I learned about Willow's biological father. She approached Carrie on a couple different occasions to ask her if she could tell you—and it was Carrie who said no. She and Emma even fought about it."

Clay took a seat on the end of the bed and set his elbows on his knees as he put his face in his hands. He was exhausted and heartsore.

He hated to think about Emma feeling this way, too.

"Carrie told Emma that all the attention had been on her for over a year—and she just wanted a bit of attention for her wedding. She didn't want this to hang over everything and detract from the festivities. To be honest, I didn't like it, and neither did Emma." Jack sat next to Clay. "The only reason Emma did what she did was to honor her sister's wishes. It was eating Emma alive—just like it was me. She was going to tell you last night, even if it meant hurting Carrie, someone she loves more than anyone else on this planet. If I had known, I would have let her."

Clay sighed. He believed Jack—and it confirmed what Emma had tried to tell him last night when he'd still been angry.

"She loves you, Clay. And she loves Willow. In the short time I've known her—and from what Carrie and her parents have told me—I know Emma to be honest, trustworthy and sacrificial. She's been hurt, just like you have, and she's doing her best to put her life back together." Jack set his hand on Clay's back. "Don't let my and Carrie's interfering keep you two from finding happiness. Because if you do, then Sadie and Tyler win."

Clay closed his eyes and let Jack's words sink into his battered heart. His cousin was right.

Emma had told him last night that she loved him, but in his stubbornness and pain, he had not acknowledged what she had said. If she was anything like him—and he suspected she was—it had taken a lot of courage to open her heart to love again. To tell him in the midst of his anger and resentment had been an even greater risk.

She deserved so much better than what he had given her last night. Her tears and vulnerability in coming to his room so soon after he had learned the truth showed him that she wanted to ease his pain and suffering.

But by turning her away, he had caused *her* pain and suffering.

"Do you love her, Clay?" Jack asked.

"I do." Clay nodded. "But I'm afraid I've messed this up."

"There's still time." Jack stood, a smile on his face. "She loves you, and that hasn't changed since last night. You need to find her and tell her how you feel."

Clay also stood, feeling energized and hopeful again. But what if Emma didn't want him anymore? What if he had hurt her so badly, she couldn't trust him with her heart? Anxiety mounted in his chest.

Jack's cell phone rang, and he grabbed it off the bedside table.

"It's the pastor," he said as he pressed the green icon. "Hello?"

Clay paced over to the window and looked out at the lawn leading to the lake. Guests were already arriving and the ushers were seating them on the white chairs. Where was Emma right now? Probably helping Carrie get ready.

"Thanks," Jack said. "I'll see you in a couple minutes." He turned off the phone and put it in his back pocket. "Pastor Ed is waiting for us in the lobby to walk out to the ceremony. He's orchestrated the timing with Emma so that she will keep Carrie in her room until we're under the arch and then the bridesmaids will bring Carrie downstairs and lead her out to the ceremony."

"So I don't have time to talk to Emma now?"

"I don't think so—but there will be time after the ceremony. You'll have all day to talk to her."

Disappointment felt heavy in Clay's chest, but he nodded. Right now it was about Jack and Carrie. Later, it could be about him and Emma.

If there was a "him and Emma." After last night, he wasn't so sure.

"Are we good?" Jack asked, searching Clay's face for an answer. "Do you forgive me?"

Clay offered Jack the first smile he'd felt like giving anyone since last night. "We're good, Jack."

"Do you think less of Carrie?"

Shaking his head, Clay said, "We all do things we regret. I know Carrie wasn't trying to hurt me. She just wanted her wedding day to be special. I'm excited for you to get married, and I wish you and Carrie every happiness possible."

Jack reached out to shake Clay's hand, but Clay pulled him into a bear hug.

If anyone deserved happiness, it was Jack.

They left the honeymoon suite and walked downstairs to the lobby, where the pastor was waiting. He grinned at them and then shook their hands.

"Ready to get married?" Pastor Ed asked Jack.

"Ready as I'll ever be." Jack's grin was infectious.

Clay was happy that everything that had happened the night before hadn't prevented Carrie and Jack from proceeding with their wedding.

They left the lodge and were greeted with a

brilliant blue sky and not a cloud in sight. The storm from the night before had left the grass greener than ever and offered a crispness to the air that was refreshing. It was a little cooler than it had been, for which Clay was thankful, too.

All he needed to do was get through the ceremony and then find a moment alone with Emma to tell her he'd been a fool. But more importantly, that he loved her, too, and didn't want the past to come between them.

He just hoped and prayed Emma could find it within her heart to forgive him.

Chapter Fifteen

Emma stood near the bedroom door, admiring Carrie in her wedding dress. It was perfect for a lakeside wedding, with a short train and clean lines. The dress was made of satin and fell from her hips straight to the floor. There were no beads, no lace, no sequins, ribbons or bows. It was an elegant gown that fit her—and the rest of the wedding—to perfection.

Earlier, Emma had taken Carrie to the kitchen and showed her the cake Clay had made. Not only had Carrie loved it but she had declared that it was better than the picture. When Carrie asked who had made it, Emma told her it had been Clay. Carrie's eyes had filled with tears, and she'd given Emma a tight hug, asking Emma to forgive her again, promising that she would apologize to Clay, too—and thank him for the beautiful cake.

"It's time for the veil," their mom said as she approached Carrie with the veil that both she and Emma had worn on their wedding days.

Emma tried not to feel emotional as she watched her mom attach the veil to Carrie's updo. She prayed that Carrie's marriage would be happier than her own—though Emma had had some very happy years in the beginning.

"Pastor Ed is taking Jack to the lake right now?" Carrie asked as she looked at Emma in the reflection of the mirror.

"Yes. They should be nearly there." Emma walked to the window and looked out at the massive lawn leading toward the lake. She could see Pastor Ed, Jack and Clay walking down the aisle between all the assembled guests.

Her heart did a little flip at seeing Clay again, though it was only his back and he was so far away. She hadn't slept well the night before, reliving all the things they had said to each other when she had been at his door. Her heart was so tender, she was afraid it would never be mended again. But she had resolved to stop thinking about it around two in the morning and decide to focus on her sister instead. The last thing she wanted was for Carrie's wedding day to be ruined, so she had fallen into a fitful sleep and had set her mind that morning not to think about Clay.

It was an impossible feat, but thankfully they had been busy getting ready all morning and she had been able to distract herself.

Her mom and sister had both wanted to know how her talk with Clay had gone the night before, and she had told them, but then she had said they were done talking about it. Carrie had seemed relieved, and their mom had only nodded in understanding and sympathy.

But now they were minutes away from the ceremony, and Emma would have to face Clay again. She didn't know how she would pretend she was okay for the next several hours as they stood across from each other during the wedding or as they sat near each other at the head table or as they gave their speeches during the meal. But somehow, she would do it for Carrie.

She turned away from the window and smiled at her sister. "Should I text Dad and let him know you're ready?"

"Would you?" Carrie was glowing today, her brown eyes shining with happiness.

Emma nodded and pulled her phone out of her purse to send their dad a quick text. He was just a few doors down and would be with them in seconds.

There were three other bridesmaids, all close friends and family, and it was Emma's job to round them up and bring them down to the lobby where the groomsmen, minus Clay, would be waiting. Emma was the only person who would walk down the aisle alone.

But on the way back, after the ceremony, she would be on Clay's arm.

She said a quick prayer for strength and then faced her sister. "You look beautiful, Carrie." She gave Carrie a hug and then offered her a smile. "I'll see you down there."

"Thanks, Em." Carrie touched Emma's shoulders. "I love you—and I'm so sorry for everything that's happened."

"I forgive you—and I told you not to worry about it anymore. This is your wedding. Let's celebrate and have some fun."

Carrie nodded.

Emma led the bridesmaids toward the door, where they crossed paths with her dad, looking handsome in his suit. He held the door open for them to pass through.

"You look lovely, Emma," he said as he kissed her cheek. "We'll be doing this again soon for you."

Even though his words had been meant to comfort her, they felt heavy and depressing as she smiled at him and then walked into the hallway.

She didn't know if she'd ever marry again—or if she'd even find true love again. Her heart belonged to Clay, and she was afraid it would never belong to anyone else. If he couldn't trust her and return her love, then she would remain single and continue the life she had created for herself since losing Tyler.

And it was a good life she had made. She lifted her chin and focused on the path ahead. Before she'd met Clay, she had been comfortable. She had friends, a good job, a great church and a welcoming community. She could find contentment again.

She would have to.

The three groomsmen and an usher were waiting in the lobby with Liv, who was giving them instructions. Their mom would walk out with the usher first, then the groomsmen and bridesmaids would follow. Emma would come next, and behind her would be Carrie and their dad. As they lined up, their mom came down the stairs and then their dad and Carrie.

Carrie had pulled the veil over her face, and she looked stunning. Emma smiled at her and took her place in line.

Liv peeked outside and then came in with a big smile. "We're ready! Let's head out."

Emma hadn't expected to be nervous, but knowing that she would face Clay made her pulse tick higher. Would he even meet her eyes? Or would he ignore her? She thought she could handle being ignored better than she could handle seeing his anger and disappointment again.

Her mom left the lodge with the usher, and the groomsmen and bridesmaids followed.

Emma gave Carrie one last smile, and then she, too, walked out into the blinding sunshine.

It took her eyes a second to adjust, and then she could see everything clearly. Almost two hundred guests had been expected, and it looked like nearly all the seats were full.

Emma clutched her bouquet of roses and followed behind the groomsmen and bridesmaids. Her dress was hunter green, and it was just as simple and elegant as Carrie's gown. It was satin, with clean lines and no frills. The white roses were tied with a simple green bow that matched the dresses.

Everyone turned to look at the wedding party as they came across the flagstone path to the water's edge. Emma couldn't get a good look at Clay or Jack yet. But she knew it would only be a few more seconds before the inevitable glance that would tell her everything.

She walked up the aisle, smiling at friends and family, and caught a glimpse of Willow in her grandma's arms. Emma hadn't seen the baby since last night—and for a second, she thought she would lose her resolve and start crying.

Willow saw Emma and reached for her. Emma smiled but had to force herself to look away. More than anything, she wanted to pull Willow into her arms and hold her—but she didn't know if she'd ever have the privilege again. Clay would probably leave right after his speech, as he'd said, and she wouldn't get to say goodbye to Willow.

Her chin quivered for a second, but she took a deep breath and focused on why she was here.

As she came to the head of the gathering, she saw the pastor and Jack—and then she saw Clay.

He looked handsome in his suit, with his dark hair combed back and his face freshly shaved. He did not avert his gaze but met Emma's—and in that instant, she knew he wasn't mad at her anymore. His beautiful brown eyes were filled with so many emotions—regret, hope, fear, longing—but not anger. They communicated so much to her in such a short amount of time, taking her breath away, but then the moment was over and she was finding her place at the head of the bridesmaids' line.

The pastor asked for the guests to rise, and the music changed as Carrie and her dad started up the aisle.

Emma's heart was pounding hard, and she wanted to look at Clay again to see if she had read his expression right or if she had only wished it to be true. But she had to watch her sister.

Everyone smiled at Carrie as she came up the aisle, and when she was finally at Jack's side, Emma let herself turn to look at Clay.

He met her gaze over Jack's shoulder, and Emma saw it again—the deep longing in his gaze, intermingled with the uncertainty.

She didn't want to waste another moment needing him to know she was sorry and wanted to make things right with him. She wasn't sure if he would respond to her while they were standing there, but she had to try.

Her lips trembled as she lifted them in a hopeful smile, trying to communicate all she could with her eyes.

And Clay smiled back.

It was all she needed for that moment, and

she had the strength to return her attention to Carrie and Jack.

The ceremony was beautiful as the sun shimmered off the lake and a gentle breeze kept the heat at bay. After the pastor gave a short sermon on marriage, Carrie and Jack shared their wedding vows and made their commitment to each other in front of their friends and family. It wasn't a long ceremony, but it was heartfelt and personal—and throughout it all, Emma and Clay shared many special glances, giving Emma hope that there was a chance he could forgive her.

When it was time to exchange the rings, Emma took Carrie's bouquet and Clay stepped forward with the rings.

The couple placed their rings on each other's fingers, and then the pastor announced they were man and wife. He told Jack to kiss his bride, and all the guests erupted in cheers and clapping.

Emma's heart felt like it might burst from happiness for her sister—and from the anticipation of walking beside Clay in a few seconds. She prayed she hadn't misunderstood his smile or his glances or the look in his eyes as Carrie reached for her bouquet.

The newly married couple were introduced, and then they walked down the aisle together.

Clay stepped forward and extended his arm to Emma. Her legs felt wobbly as she joined him and slipped her arm through his.

He drew her close, and she inhaled the fragrance he wore, savoring the feel of his body next to hers.

"I'm sorry, Emma," he said for her ears only as they started down the aisle to follow Carrie and Jack. "Will you forgive me?"

"There's nothing to forgive," she whispered.

"I acted poorly last night, and you didn't deserve it."

Emma smiled at everyone she passed, though her thoughts and emotions were with Clay and his words.

Carrie and Jack stood ready to receive their guests, so Emma broke away from Clay's side as she hugged her sister and then Jack, wishing them all the best. Clay did the same.

Soon there were others taking up Carrie and Jack's focus, and Clay turned to Emma, offering her his full attention.

"Can we go somewhere and talk?" he asked. "We won't be needed at the reception for a little while."

Emma nodded. "The garden isn't too far

from here." It was the same garden where she had talked with her mom the night before and would offer them the best privacy. Carrie and Jack wouldn't even know they were missing.

They followed the flagstone path where it diverged, and were soon away from the prying eyes of anyone who might have noticed them slip away. Trees came up all around them, blocking them from view.

Clay walked close beside Emma, but he didn't take her hand or reach out to her again. Her nerves returned, and she was afraid of what he might say. He could be sorry—and still not want to pursue a future together.

The very thought made her shiver, despite the heat.

When they arrived in the garden, Emma walked over to the bench and took a seat, thankful to be off her wobbly legs. She set her bouquet on the bench next to her, afraid that her trembling hands would make the flowers shake.

Clay sat beside her, and for a second, they just looked at one another.

Then he gently reached out and took her hand, causing it to become still again.

His touch was all she needed to know that he still cared about her, and she went into his arms.

"Emma," he whispered against her cheek.

"I'm so sorry for last night. I was a fool to think you could have purposefully hurt me."

"And I was a fool to keep the truth from you. I'm sorry, too, Clay. If I could do it all over again, I would tell you." Her heart was pounding so hard, she was certain he could feel it against his chest. "I love you," she whispered. "And I would never try to hurt you or Willow."

He pulled back and placed his hands on either side of her face. "I should have told you last night that I love you, too, Emma. It is the greatest honor of my life that you would entrust your heart to me, and I promise you I will never neglect it again. You have my word."

A smile tilted Emma's mouth. "You love me?"

The look in his eyes was all she needed, but his tender words sealed the truth in her heart. "I love you, Emma Holt, and I want to kiss you." He grinned, removing all trace of uncertainty and pain. He rested his forehead against hers. "I've wanted to kiss you for days now."

"Then kiss me," she whispered.

He lowered his lips to hers and wrapped his arms around her, pulling her close. His lips were soft and tender but filled with a passion that took her breath away.

Emma slipped her arms around his neck, encouraging him to deepen the kiss as she drew him closer.

He groaned, and his arms tightened around her waist.

When he finally pulled back, breathless, he smiled down at her. "That was better than I had hoped."

She returned his smile with one of her own. "And it will only get better from here."

"Promise?" he asked.

"I promise." And Emma didn't make promises lightly.

Epilogue

Clay stood in the kitchen and stared out the window to his new backyard. A large lawn sloped down to the Mississippi River, which was low for this time of year and fringed on either side by colorful trees that had begun to turn for fall.

It felt good to finally be in his new home after three months of searching for just the right house. The only thing that would make it better was having Emma and Willow with him.

"Clay?" Emma called from the foyer. "We're here."

He grinned at the sound of her voice. He would never get tired of hearing it or of seeing her again after being apart. Granted, it had only been twenty minutes since she had left to pick Willow up from the babysitter—but even twenty minutes was too long.

Clay would have gone to get Willow with Emma, but the movers had still been there and he'd needed to direct them with his furniture and boxes. The work was half-done, but now that everything was in the new house, he was eager to get settled.

But at the moment, he wanted to be with Emma and Willow.

Emma had Willow on her hip and was setting down her diaper bag when Clay walked into the foyer. They both turned to look at him, and it struck him all over again that he was blessed beyond compare.

"There are my girls!" he said.

"I think she likes the new house." Emma stood on tiptoe and kissed Clay.

He put his arms around her to return it, and then he kissed Willow's head.

"Thank you for getting her," he said.

"It wasn't any trouble." Emma handed Willow over to Clay. "She was happy to see me."

"We're all happy to see you." He winked at her and then lifted Willow in the air, which elicited a delightful squeal from his daughter. "She might not know it now," he said to Emma, "but this house will be the center of her world for the next eighteen years."

Moving boxes were piled high along the

walls of the foyer and in each of the rooms. The house was large but cozy, with lots of space for Willow to grow.

It had taken about three months for Clay to sell his house in St. Cloud and close on the new one in Timber Falls. Emma had helped him look for just the right neighborhood and just the right house. She knew the neighbors to the north. Drew and Whitney Keelen were a couple Emma had met at church when she'd moved to Timber Falls, and she had introduced to Clay when he had visited. Their adopted son, Elliot, was seventeen months old, and their baby girl, Daphne, was six months. They would be the perfect playmates for Willow, who was now nine months.

Clay held Willow on his hip as he put his other arm around Emma's waist and led her into the living room to their left. The couches had been brought in and placed against two different walls, though Clay would move them to fit the space better. He was eager to get Emma's opinion about where she thought they'd look best.

He wanted her opinion about everything he did in the house.

"Are you going to start unpacking right away?" Emma asked as the three of them sat on the couch facing the fireplace.

"There's time enough for that later," he said

as he pulled her close. "I could use a little break."

They had spent weeks packing up Clay's house in St. Cloud, and through it all, Emma had been by his side. She had helped him find childcare in Timber Falls and had taken care of most of the arrangements for the move. She'd been there with him all day, directing the movers, organizing the boxes and cleaning out drawers and cabinets. She needed a break, too.

"I don't know what I would have done without you," he said as he kissed Emma again.

She snuggled next to him as Willow gnawed on a wooden teething ring in her hands.

When Willow noticed they were both looking at her, she grinned, showing off her two bottom teeth. Drool dripped off her chin, and Emma reached out and wiped it away.

In the three months since Jack and Carrie's wedding, Emma had become the most important person in Willow and Clay's life. They spent almost every day together, getting to know one another better, discovering the little idiosyncrasies that made up their personalities.

And Clay loved her more and more with each passing day. He'd been sure at the wedding that she would be the love of his life—but as the months had passed, he had become certain that she would also be his best friend.

"If you're not going to unpack," she said, "what would you like to do this evening?"

"I thought we should order a pizza and watch a movie together," he said.

She smiled and looked up at him. "You know what happens when we watch movies."

He returned her smile. "We cuddle."

And they kissed—because Clay couldn't be that close to Emma and not want to kiss her.

Emma laughed and let out a happy sigh. "I would love to eat pizza and watch a movie tonight. It's been a busy week."

Besides helping him move, Emma was still a full-time nurse practitioner and kept a busy schedule.

"It's a good thing tomorrow is Saturday and you can sleep in."

"And now that you live in Timber Falls," she added, "I only have to drive across town, instead of make a thirty-minute trip home." She laid her head on his shoulder and picked up the teething ring that Willow had dropped. "Another thing to be thankful for."

Clay glanced over at the end table and saw a small box lying there. "That's strange," he said.

Emma lifted her head. "What?"

"The movers must have put this box in the wrong room." He reached over and lifted it off the table, balancing Willow on his lap.

"Where does it belong?" Emma asked.

Clay handed the black velvet box to Emma and said, "On your finger."

She sat up straight and looked from the ring box to Clay, her lips parting. "What is this?"

He grinned, his pulse picking up speed. He'd been planning this moment for weeks, waiting impatiently to finally own the home where he hoped he, Emma and Willow could start over. He'd wanted to be in the house they would call their own when he finally asked her to marry him.

The day had arrived at last.

"Willow and I have a question for you," he said. "One we've been waiting a long time to ask."

Emma's eyes filled with tears as she pressed her lips together.

"Are you going to open the box?" he asked her quietly.

She nodded as a tear slipped down her cheek. Slowly, Emma opened the ring box, and her eyes lit up with pleasure.

"Clay," she whispered, "it's beautiful."

"I hoped you'd like it. Willow helped me pick it out."

Emma giggled and cried as she lifted the diamond ring out of the box and held it up to the sunshine coming in at the window. It sparkled.

"I love it," she said. "It's perfect."

Clay held Willow as he took the ring from Emma and slowly got off the couch. He bent to his knee, so that he was eye level with Emma.

The baby looked at him but didn't seem to think anything was strange.

"Emma Alexandrea Holt," Clay said as he took her left hand in his. "Will you marry me and be Willow's mama?"

More tears fell from Emma's eyes as she nodded. "Yes," she said. "I will marry you and be Willow's mama."

Clay grinned and slipped the ring onto Emma's ring finger. It fit perfectly, just like she fit perfectly in Clay and Willow's life.

He stood and helped her to her feet, then he wrapped his arms around her and Willow and held them close.

"I love you, Em," he said as he leaned down and kissed her.

Willow put her wet hand on Clay's cheek and giggled, causing him to pull back from Emma.

He and Emma both laughed, causing Willow to laugh, too.

"I love you, too, Clay," Emma said. "I can't wait to marry you and become a family."

"We already are a family," he told her. "We just need to make it official."

"Let's do it as soon as possible. I'm tired of leaving you two every night to go to my own house."

"And we're tired of it, too," he said. "I want you to make this home yours. We can paint the walls any color you'd like and set up the rooms however you want. You can throw out all my furniture and move your own in, too, if that's how you want it."

"I like your furniture," she said as she looked around the living room. "It will match mine perfectly."

He grinned. "Let's order some pizza and pick out a movie. The rest can wait for a different day."

"I like the sound of that."

They went into the kitchen where Clay had left his cell phone. After they ordered pizza, they went up to Willow's new room and set up her crib, making sure everything was in place for her to feel comfortable and safe for her first night in the new home.

An hour later, after they finished their supper, they gave Willow a bath and put her to bed, then they went into the living room and cuddled up on the couch to watch a movie.

As Clay held Emma in his arms, he couldn't help but count his blessings.

At the top of his list was his bride-to-be.

Their lives had been inextricably woven together through heartbreak and betrayal, but through God's grace and perfect timing, they had found joy and happiness once again.

* * * * *

If you liked this story from Gabrielle Meyer, check out her previous Love Inspired books:

A Mother's Secret
Unexpected Christmas Joy
A Home for Her Baby
Snowed in for Christmas
Fatherhood Lessons
The Soldier's Baby Promise
The Baby Proposal

Available now from Love Inspired!
Find more great reads at
www.LoveInspired.com

Dear Reader,

It was fun to return to the fictional resort at Lakepoint Lodge on the shores of Lake Madeline, which first appeared in *Snowed in for Christmas*. Though the resort and lake do not exist in real life, they are a compilation of lakes and resorts in Minnesota that I love. I have sat among the pines in outdoor chapels, sung around many campfires near the water and moored a boat on several islands. These are the bits and pieces of my own life that I love to share in my stories, and I hope you've enjoyed them.

Happy reading!
Gabrielle Meyer

Get 3 FREE REWARDS!

We'll send you 2 FREE Books plus a FREE Mystery Gift.

FREE Value Over $20

Both the **Love Inspired**® and **Love Inspired**® Suspense series feature compelling novels filled with inspirational romance, faith, forgiveness and hope.

YES! Please send me 2 FREE novels from the Love Inspired or Love Inspired Suspense series and my FREE gift (gift is worth about $10 retail). After receiving them, if I don't wish to receive any more books, I can return the shipping statement marked "cancel." If I don't cancel, I will receive 6 brand-new Love Inspired Larger-Print books or Love Inspired Suspense Larger-Print books every month and be billed just $6.49 each in the U.S. or $6.74 each in Canada. That is a savings of at least 16% off the cover price. It's quite a bargain! Shipping and handling is just 50¢ per book in the U.S. and $1.25 per book in Canada.* I understand that accepting the 2 free books and gift places me under no obligation to buy anything. I can always return a shipment and cancel at any time by calling the number below. The free books and gift are mine to keep no matter what I decide.

Choose one: ☐ **Love Inspired Larger-Print** (122/322 BPA GRPA)   ☐ **Love Inspired Suspense Larger-Print** (107/307 BPA GRPA)   ☐ **Or Try Both!** (122/322 & 107/307 BPA GRRP)

Name (please print)

Address   Apt. #

City   State/Province   Zip/Postal Code

Email: Please check this box ☐ if you would like to receive newsletters and promotional emails from Harlequin Enterprises ULC and its affiliates. You can unsubscribe anytime.

Mail to the Harlequin Reader Service:
IN U.S.A.: P.O. Box 1341, Buffalo, NY 14240-8531
IN CANADA: P.O. Box 603, Fort Erie, Ontario L2A 5X3

Want to try 2 free books from another series? Call 1-800-873-8635 or visit www.ReaderService.com.

---

*Terms and prices subject to change without notice. Prices do not include sales taxes, which will be charged (if applicable) based on your state or country of residence. Canadian residents will be charged applicable taxes. Offer not valid in Quebec. This offer is limited to one order per household. Books received may not be as shown. Not valid for current subscribers to the Love Inspired or Love Inspired Suspense series. All orders subject to approval. Credit or debit balances in a customer's account(s) may be offset by any other outstanding balance owed by or to the customer. Please allow 4 to 6 weeks for delivery. Offer available while quantities last.

Your Privacy—Your information is being collected by Harlequin Enterprises ULC, operating as Harlequin Reader Service. For a complete summary of the information we collect, how we use this information and to whom it is disclosed, please visit our privacy notice located at corporate.harlequin.com/privacy-notice. From time to time we may also exchange your personal information with reputable third parties. If you wish to opt out of this sharing of your personal information, please visit readerservice.com/consumerschoice or call 1-800-873-8635. **Notice to California Residents**—Under California law, you have specific rights to control and access your data. For more information on these rights and how to exercise them, visit corporate.harlequin.com/california-privacy.

LIRLIS23

Get 3 FREE REWARDS!

We'll send you 2 FREE Books plus a FREE Mystery Gift.

FREE
Value Over
$20

Both the **Harlequin® Special Edition** and **Harlequin® Heartwarming™** series feature compelling novels filled with stories of love and strength where the bonds of friendship, family and community unite.

YES! Please send me 2 FREE novels from the Harlequin Special Edition or Harlequin Heartwarming series and my FREE Gift (gift is worth about $10 retail). After receiving them, if I don't wish to receive any more books, I can return the shipping statement marked "cancel." If I don't cancel, I will receive 6 brand-new Harlequin Special Edition books every month and be billed just $5.49 each in the U.S. or $6.24 each in Canada, a savings of at least 12% off the cover price, or 4 brand-new Harlequin Heartwarming Larger-Print books every month and be billed just $6.24 each in the U.S. or $6.74 each in Canada, a savings of at least 19% off the cover price. It's quite a bargain! Shipping and handling is just 50¢ per book in the U.S. and $1.25 per book in Canada.* I understand that accepting the 2 free books and gift places me under no obligation to buy anything. I can always return a shipment and cancel at any time by calling the number below. The free books and gift are mine to keep no matter what I decide.

Choose one:
☐ **Harlequin Special Edition**
(235/335 BPA GRMK)

☐ **Harlequin Heartwarming Larger-Print**
(161/361 BPA GRMK)

☐ **Or Try Both!**
(235/335 & 161/361 BPA GRPZ)

Name (please print)

Address   Apt. #

City   State/Province   Zip/Postal Code

Email: Please check this box ☐ if you would like to receive newsletters and promotional emails from Harlequin Enterprises ULC and its affiliates. You can unsubscribe anytime.

Mail to the Harlequin Reader Service:
IN U.S.A.: P.O. Box 1341, Buffalo, NY 14240-8531
IN CANADA: P.O. Box 603, Fort Erie, Ontario L2A 5X3

Want to try 2 free books from another series! Call **1-800-873-8635** or visit www.ReaderService.com.

*Terms and prices subject to change without notice. Prices do not include sales taxes, which will be charged (if applicable) based on your state or country of residence. Canadian residents will be charged applicable taxes. Offer not valid in Quebec. This offer is limited to one order per household. Books received may not be as shown. Not valid for current subscribers to the Harlequin Special Edition or Harlequin Heartwarming series. All orders subject to approval. Credit or debit balances in a customer's account(s) may be offset by any other outstanding balance owed by or to the customer. Please allow 4 to 6 weeks for delivery. Offer available while quantities last.

Your Privacy—Your information is being collected by Harlequin Enterprises ULC, operating as Harlequin Reader Service. For a complete summary of the information we collect, how we use this information and to whom it is disclosed, please visit our privacy notice located at corporate.harlequin.com/privacy-notice. From time to time we may also exchange your personal information with reputable third parties. If you wish to opt out of this sharing of your personal information, please visit readerservice.com/consumerschoice or call 1-800-873-8635. **Notice to California Residents**—Under California law, you have specific rights to control and access your data. For more information on these rights and how to exercise them, visit corporate.harlequin.com/california-privacy.

HSEHW23

COMING NEXT MONTH FROM
Love Inspired

THE AMISH MARRIAGE ARRANGEMENT
Amish Country Matches • by Patricia Johns

Sarai Peachy is convinced that her *grossmammi* and their next-door neighbor are the perfect match. But the older man's grandson isn't so sure. When a storm forces the two to work together on repairs, will spending time with Arden Stoltzfus prove to Sarai that the former heartbreaker is a changed man?

THE AMISH NANNY'S PROMISE
by Amy Grochowski

Since the loss of his wife, Nick Weaver has relied on nanny Fern Beiler to care for him and his *kinner*. But when the community pushes them into a marriage of convenience, the simple arrangement grows more complicated. Will these two friends find love for a lifetime?

HER ALASKAN COMPANION
K-9 Companions • by Heidi McCahan

Moving to Alaska is the fresh start that pregnant widow Lexi Thomas has been looking for. But taking care of a rambunctious dog wasn't part of the plan. When an unlikely friendship blooms between her and the dog's owner, Heath Donovan, can she take a chance and risk her heart again?

THE RELUCTANT RANCHER
Lone Star Heritage • by Jolene Navarro

World-weary FBI agent Enzo Flores returns home to help his pregnant sister. When she goes into premature labor, he needs help to care for his nephew and the ranch. Will childhood rival Resa Espinoza step in to help and forgive their troubled past?

FALLING FOR THE FAMILY NEXT DOOR
Sage Creek • by Jennifer Slattery

Needing a fresh start, Daria Ellis moves to Texas with her niece and nephew. But it's more challenging than she ever imagined, especially with handsome cowboy Tyler Reyes living next door. When they clash over property lines, will it ruin everything or prove to be a blessing in disguise?

A HAVEN FOR HIS TWINS
by April Arrington

Deciding to right the wrongs of the past, former bull rider Holt Williams returns home to reclaim his twin sons. But Jessie Alden, the woman who's raised them all these years, isn't keen on the idea. Can he be trusted, or will he hurt his sons—and her—all over again?

LOOK FOR THESE AND OTHER LOVE INSPIRED BOOKS WHEREVER BOOKS ARE SOLD, INCLUDING MOST BOOKSTORES, SUPERMARKETS, DISCOUNT STORES AND DRUGSTORES.

LICNM0623

HARLEQUIN
PLUS

Try the best multimedia
subscription service for romance
readers like you!

Read, Watch and Play.

Experience the easiest way to get
the romance content you crave.

Start your **FREE TRIAL** at
<u>www.harlequinplus.com/freetrial</u>.